PRAISE F
ANNABELLE DIXON COZY MYSTERY
SERIES

"Absolutely wonderful!!"
"Another winner. Loved it. Can't wait for the next one."
"I couldn't put it down!"
"Best book yet, Alison. I'm not kidding. You did a heck of a job."
"I read it that night, and it was GREAT!"
"Grab it and read it, my friends."
"A real page turner and a perfect cozy mystery."
"As a former village vicar this ticks the box for me."
"I enjoyed this book from the first line to the last page."
"Annabelle, with her great intuition, caring personality, yet imperfect judgement, is a wonderful main character."
"It's fun to grab a cup of tea and pretend I'm sitting in the vicarage discussing the latest mysteries with Annabelle whilst she polishes off the last of the cupcakes."
"Great book - love Reverend Annabelle Dixon and can't wait to read more of her books."
"Annabelle reminds me of Agatha Christie's Miss Marple."
"A perfect weekend read."
"Terrific cozy mystery!"

KILLER AT THE CULT

BOOKS IN THE REVEREND ANNABELLE DIXON SERIES

Fireworks in France

KILLER AT THE CULT

ALISON GOLDEN

JAMIE VOUGEOT

Published by Mesa Verde Publishing
P.O. Box 1002
San Carlos, CA 94070

ISBN: 978-0988795518

To my boys who have allowed me to fly. Now it is your turn.

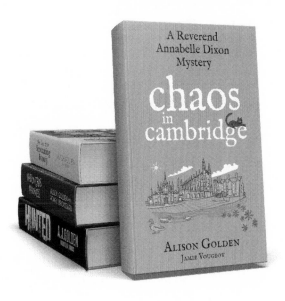

"Your emails seem to come on days when I need to read them because they are so upbeat."
- Linda W -

For a limited time, you can get the first books in each of my series - *Chaos in Cambridge, Hunted* (exclusively for subscribers - not available anywhere else), *The Case of the Screaming Beauty, and Mardi Gras Madness* - plus updates about new releases, promotions, and other Insider exclusives, by signing up for my mailing list at:

https://www.alisongolden.com/annabelle

CHAPTER ONE

ANNABELLE SMELT THE sticky, sugary scent as it wafted over her. She shifted uncomfortably in her seat. To her left, slices of chocolate caramel shortcake lay piled in a mound the shape of a pyramid. Cherry Bakewells, their soft, white icing topped by a single, red glacé dot stared at her. A light brown coffee sponge, its ganache filling oozing at the edges, stood majestically next to them, powdered sugar and walnuts elegantly sprinkled across its surface. Round lemon tarts lay like replica suns on a vintage blue and white plate, accented by orange slices and bright green leaves, whilst a succulent sunken apple cake glinted when the light caught it.

Annabelle had snagged a table next to the window display at Flynn's tea shop, a decision she now realised hadn't been her best. The sweets were imprisoned beneath clear glass domes but when her nostrils weren't being assailed, her eyes watered with the temptation she was desperately trying to hold at bay. She looked outside as she waited for the sweet aroma to pass. It was Saturday, and the tearoom was busy. She pressed her lips together and fingered a teaspoon as she waited for her tea to brew.

After a minute, Annabelle lifted the Union Jack cosy covering her teapot and, placing a forefinger on the lid, efficiently poured tea into her china cup. She blew across the surface of the hot, almost orange liquid, making ripples in the surface. The warm, damp, steamy response made her nose tickle. She sighed and looked out of the window again, propping her elbows on the table and ignoring her mother's admonishments that bounced around her head. Her hands cradled the elegant, eggshell blue cup decorated with yellow and red flowers. She took a sip. The taste made her smile as she thought of her father, a London cabbie, who when taking his first drink of tea after a hard night's work on the city's streets, would smack his lips and say, "Good cup of tea, that. Put hairs on yer chest."

It was a beautiful day, the sun shone. The villagers wore shorts and T-shirts. They were out in force, making the most of the gorgeous mid-June weather. It was market day, and the stalls were set up in the village square. Ernie Plumber, the greengrocer, was barking out prices. Colourful fruit and vegetables were laid out on his produce stall as they had been for decades. Veg lay to the right, fruit to the left; apples and cauliflowers at the back, strawberries, peas, and broad beans in front. Annabelle doubted Mr. Plumber had changed the configuration of his stall in the twenty-five years he'd been working the market. And good for him, she thought, his customers knew just what to expect. Routine and stability were what the locals liked about their village.

The Upton St. Mary chapter of the Women's Institute was an exception to that rule. Right next to the greengrocer's stall the WI had set out their homemade cakes and jars of honey and jam. They lay on a linen-covered table with pamphlets about the chapter's speakers' schedule splayed in a neat fan next to them. Annabelle made a mental note to talk about that to the ladies manning the table. Given the precise arrangement of the leaflets, the vicar knew from experience that no one would dare pick any of them up, no one would ruin such a perfect display. No one would learn that Mr. Nancarrow from the undertakers would give a talk next month on how to transform burial ashes into jewellery or of the repeat outing to the Twisted Butterfly studio for a pole dancing class.

The earlier WI trip to the Twisted Butterfly had caused quite a stir. A few women, headed by Philippa, her church secretary and housekeeper, had come to Annabelle to urge her to *do something*. They were a small yet vocal bunch, but they had left Annabelle's cottage dissatisfied, her advice to consider it an "extreme yoga class" buzzing in their ears.

Veteran WI members Mrs. Gates and Mrs. Polwerrin sat on stools behind their table nattering. They only interrupted their conversation when elderly Mrs. Freneweth paused to show interest in their cakes. The WI ladies welcomed her, beaming at their prospective customer. They were proud of their wares and loved to show them off. From her vantage point, Annabelle was confident that pleasantries would be exchanged, compliments about the cakes would be paid, and surprise would be expressed over their modest cost. Money would then be exchanged, and the customer would eventually shuffle off, marvelling at the bargain they'd just scored. When she got home, Mrs. Freneweth would no doubt reward herself with a lovely sit-down, a slice of her newly purchased cake, and her beverage of choice.

As she watched the scene playing out just as she had anticipated, the cake in question being a pale yellow Victoria sandwich, Annabelle's mind wandered to Inspector Nicholls. Mike. He liked a jam and buttercream filling too.

CHAPTER TWO

ANNABELLE'S THOUGHTS WERE interrupted when her table was jolted forcefully, sloshing the tea in her cup. She quickly lifted her elbows from the table to steady her hands as the china on the table tinkled.

"Billy, watch what you're doing! You nearly spilt the vicar's tea!" Mrs. Breville let out an exasperated sigh. "Sorry, Reverend," she said, shaking her head and rolling her eyes simultaneously.

Annabelle straightened the starched tablecloth. "It's perfectly fine, Mrs. Breville. No harm done."

Annabelle regarded the cause of Jeannette Breville's frustration carefully. "But what have you been doing with yourself, Billy?" The ten-year-old boy had a purple and black shiner and a graze above his eyebrow. Both arms were in slings.

"Ah, it's nothing, Annabelle."

His mother nudged him. "It's "Reverend" to you, Billy."

"Ah, Reverend, sorry. Took a tumble. From Big Boy."

"Who?"

"Big Boy, the new pony at Tinsley's." Tinsley's was the local riding school.

"Gracious me, looks like it was a little more than a tumble, Billy."

"Nah, was my own fault. Didn't grip with my knees hard enough." Billy lifted one arm to scratch his face, and Annabelle saw the plaster cast wrapped around his hand and wrist. "Fair bounced, I did. Dad always did say horses were dangerous."

"Really?"

"Have a mind of their own, see? He'd prefer I ride motorbikes. When I'm older, of course," he added, "but that always makes Mum cry."

Annabelle stared at him nonplussed. She had a tendency to agree with Billy's dad up to the part about the motorcycle. "Well, please be careful, Billy. We need you in one piece for the show, don't forget, and your mum and dad need you for a lot longer than that!"

She gave the boy a quick rub on his head, the only part of him she could find uninjured. Billy was to play the role of Pharaoh in the village's performance of the story of Joseph and his coat of many colours. Annabelle was directing.

When Billy and his mother moved off, Annabelle's attention returned to the scene outside her window. The villagers milling around the market stalls had been joined by some strangers, two women Annabelle hadn't seen before. The women were handing out flowers or trying to. The locals seemed to be employing various tactics to avoid them. Eyes were downcast, backs were turned, mothers put protective hands on their children's shoulders to guide them away even as the youngsters stopped to stare. One villager even spoke to the two women angrily when they tried to press a flower on him, lifting his hand as though he had a flea in his ear.

Annabelle frowned. The women didn't seem unpleasant, their faces were open and friendly. One of them wore a long, print skirt almost to the floor, a crinkled loose cotton top, and flat, strappy sandals. The other was dressed in working clothes, a pair of sturdy cotton trousers and a tartan flannel shirt, warm for such a midsummer day. The woman had topped it with a canvas jacket. A gardening belt full of pouches and pockets lay around her waist.

Katie Flynn, the teashop's owner, walked up to Annabelle's table. "Is there anything else I can get you, Reverend? Any cake today?"

The sugary scent emanating from the display of cakes in the window to Annabelle's left was still tempting her, but she tamped down the urge to indulge.

"No, thank you, Katie," she said, patting her stomach. "I'm trying to be good."

Katie laughed. "You're a vicar, Reverend. You can't not be good."

"Oh, I don't know about that. I can be tempted by a good slice of Devil's Food Cake as easily as anyone, as you well know. Katie, do you know who those people are? The ones with the flowers?" She pointed to the two women who were now trying to talk to the ladies from the Women's Institute. Mrs. Gates and Mrs. Polwerrin were engaged in the very English dance of trying extremely hard not to be rude whilst obviously wishing they were a thousand miles away.

"Oh, they're the people from the big house outside the village. The one at the end of Lolly Lane, past Oakcombe Cottage and the Hamiltons."

"What're they doing? They seem to be handing out flowers and talking to people."

"Yeah, they do that. Or try to. They ask for money. Sometimes they set up a table to sell stuff. They even put one up outside the newsagents last week until Frank Hammett shooed them off. And they have some kind of paper they try to sell too. I'm not sure they're very successful. People around here aren't into what they're into."

Annabelle swivelled in her chair, her eyes wide. "And what's that?"

Katie shrugged. "Not too sure, meself. They've never come in here. I'd send them away if they did. I'm not having them bothering my customers. I just know they come in on market days and hang around."

"Hmm. Interesting." Annabelle looked again at the WI women. The two strangers were still engaging them, but Mrs. Gates was standing now, pointing across the street. Mrs. Polwerrin was hard at work rearranging pamphlets that didn't need rearranging.

"What do I owe you?" Annabelle smiled at Katie and fished about in her cassock folds for some money.

"It's on the house, Vicar. Don't trouble yourself, it was just a cup of tea. Come back and see us later in the week. You're always welcome."

Katie cleared Annabelle's table and disappeared into the kitchen at the back of the teashop. By this time, Annabelle's fishing had transformed into a deep dive. Finally, she wrestled a few coins onto the table. She left them as a tip.

Annabelle brushed aside the hair that had fallen into her eyes and stood to walk out, bidding her fellow tea drinkers goodbye as she weaved her way carefully through tables laden with porcelain and hot, brown liquid. With her flowing cassock skirts, a busy tearoom was a potential disaster zone.

When she reached the street, mercifully without incident, Annabelle looked around. It was close to midday, and the market was quieting down after the mid-morning rush. She caught sight of the two women, now talking to two men who were easily distinguishable from the villagers by their embroidered smocked shirts, knickerbockers, and scraped-back, tiny braided ponytails. No self-respecting Upton St. Mary villager would be seen in garb like that unless they were morris men.

Annabelle pondered the idea that they might, indeed, be local folk dancers in traditional costume but she couldn't see any wooden sticks or bells, or an accordion for that matter. *Pity*, she thought. She enjoyed a good jig as much as the next person, although when morris dancers cracked their wooden batons together, it made her wince. One slip and someone would get a nasty bruise. She momentarily thought back to Billy Breville.

As she regarded the group, something about the woman with the working clothes caught Annabelle's eye. She squinted to peer closer. The woman was carrying a grey, white, and brown rabbit in her pocket. Annabelle recognised the breed. It was a small, lop-eared rabbit. She had had one as a pet when she was a girl. Its small head with its big, black eyes poked out of its canvas home, its nose bobbing up and down, its oversized bunny ears splayed out. Shrewdly or not, Annabelle couldn't decide which, the rabbit sat at eye level with the children that passed. They noticed it immediately. Annabelle watched as a villager and her young daughter walked past the group.

"Mummy!"

"Hmm?"

"There's a rabbit in that lady's pocket."

"Of course there is, Summer."

"No, there is, Mummy. I want to go and look."

"We don't have time."

"But M-u-m-m-y!"

Flustered, the woman took the girl's hand and pulled her along as her daughter continued to glance back the way she had come, unable to take her eye off the sight of the cute, winsome bunny. Annabelle's heart hurt a little as she watched. She felt for both mother and daughter, their relationship disrupted by their competing urges.

The church bells rang out, and Annabelle gathered herself. Bell-ringing practice. She needed to get home. She'd ask Philippa about these newcomers inspiring so much gossip and perhaps trouble. She was certain her church secretary would know all about them, probably too much. And Philippa would be only too pleased to share her opinion on the subject.

CHAPTER THREE

ANNABELLE SHUT THE door to her cottage with a bang.

"Philippa! Philippa!" she called. "Are you here?" The heavenly smell of freshly baked cupcakes drifting towards her from the kitchen announced that Philippa was indeed there.

The older woman's face popped out from behind the back door. "Cooee, Reverend. Just doing some sweeping. Gardener man has been here doing the grass, and there's cuttings all over the steps."

"Oh, well, never mind that. Finish what you're doing, and I'll put the kettle on. I want to chat to you about something." Annabelle bustled about, putting the kettle on to boil and warming the teapot. She set a tray with cups and saucers, milk but no sugar. Neither she nor Philippa took it in their tea any longer. They were both being "good." The smell of the cupcakes, though, was a distraction. Annabelle opened the cupboard to get some plates but closed it again and resolved to sit outside where the temptation would be less. More tea would help.

"You're tormenting me, Philippa," she said as she took the tea tray outside. Two young dogs, Molly and Magic, ran up to her, their brown tails wagging at one end, their pink tongues hanging out at the other.

"Whoa, doggies, you'll make me spill my tea." Annabelle set the tray down on the bench and made a fuss of the two dogs, who, once they realised she had nothing for them, returned to playing with one another in a shady corner populated by purple foxgloves, pink hydrangea, and two crabapple trees.

"What's that?" Philippa said as she moved some planters back into position. She walked over to where Annabelle was now sitting.

"The cupcakes you've made. The ones currently sitting in the oven. You know I'm trying to be good."

"You're always good, Reverend, you're a vicar." Philippa laughed. "Anyhow, those aren't for you. They're a rehearsal snack for the children, we need to keep their strength up. You're putting them through their paces with all that singing. Audrey Beamish says her daughter sings from the moment she gets up to the moment she goes to bed. That takes a lot of energy, that does."

"And demands a lot of patience from the rest of her family, I shouldn't wonder," Annabelle replied.

"There are some very high notes, to be sure. I can hear her from two streets away."

Annabelle's idea to stage the story of Joseph and his fabulous coat had initially been a modest one. She'd envisaged a few songs and an equal number of children but with the unbridled enthusiasm and imagination of the villagers, the project had developed into a major production. It now encompassed the entire songbook, virtually all the under-fifteens in the village, and an army of parents who were managing everything from building sets to making costumes, from printing programs to plastering on makeup. Everyone was talking about it, and their expectations were causing Annabelle, who'd taken on the role of producer, director, and occasional cast member, a myriad of sleepless nights. She was taking to her knees a lot. Prayer would get her through. Or so she told herself.

"I must say that the last time I dropped by, it looked like primary school playtime with all that running and shouting, but I'm sure you know what you're doing. Organised chaos, wouldn't you say?" Philippa said optimistically.

In Annabelle's experience, rehearsals erred far more on the side of chaos than organised. She had had to break up a fight during the last one. The idea of adding Philippa's sugary treats to the mix didn't bear thinking about. The children didn't need *more* energy.

"Listen, Philippa, I saw some people today in the market square. Two women. They were handing out flowers to passersby. Do you know anything about them?"

Philippa sniffed. "Would these be the people hanging around bothering folk? Enticing them with flowers and animals, using the children to trick the parents into a conversation about their blasphemous views?"

"Well, yes. Although—"

"The men who wear funny trousers?"

"Um, yes, but—"

"No one wearing trousers like that can be up to any good, Vicar. And who knows what those women hide up their flowing skirts."

"Well, no perhaps not, Philippa. But what do you know about them?"

"They're heathens, Reverend. They have strange ways. They live in the big house at the end of Lolly Lane. I've heard all kinds of stories of funny goings-on. Mr. and Mrs. Cuddy, who live at the end of the lane, say they've heard yelling and hollering at all times of the day and night. And the food they eat! All plants, you know?"

"I see, well—"

"Vegans, I think they call themselves. But it can't be good for you, can it? We're not cows, are we?"

"That's certainly unusual, however—"

"But see, they're clever. They worm their way under people's skin. Start out all nice, chatty, and before you know it, you're imprisoned in some kind of cult you can't escape from!"

"I'm sure it's not as bad as that, Philippa. You're exaggerating, surely?"

"I don't think so, Vicar. Charlie Bishop went to the house for a cup of tea and barely came away with his life! They wanted him to stay for dinner, but you know how he likes his meat."

Annabelle fought back painful memories of the hot dog eating competition they'd held at the last church fête. Charlie had been the undisputed winner and also the first in line at the doctor's surgery the next morning.

"I'd stay well away if I were you," Philippa finished.

"Hmm, it all seems rather mysterious, certainly."

"Cooee!" Barbara Simpson from the Dog and Duck clicked the gate shut and waved as she tottered up the garden path in her leopard print stilettos.

"Hello, Barbara. How are you?" Annabelle said.

"Fine, Vicar, fine. Just popped by with some of my old makeup. I thought you might be needing it for the show." She handed Annabelle a large bag of cosmetics. Palettes of eye shadows and tubes of lipsticks with evocative names such as Blastin' Blue and Opulent Orange assailed

Annabelle's eyeballs. Glitter and shimmer featured strongly in the selection.

"Thank you, Barbara, that's very generous of you." Annabelle looked down at the bag. "The false eyelashes in particular will come in very handy."

"We were just talking about the cult people from the house at the end of Lolly Lane," Philippa said.

"Ooh yes, Vicar. They're a bad lot, they are. Been coming into my pub, handing out their flowers, they have. I shoo them out sharpish."

Philippa sat up straighter and wagged her forefinger at Annabelle, invigorated now she had an ally. "I think they've brought bad blood into the village. Ever since they arrived, things have been happening."

"Like what, Philippa? Come on, tell me. I'm sure it's not as bad as all that," Annabelle said.

"Well, there was that business between Demelza Trevern and her cousin, Angie," Philippa said.

"That was a fight waiting to happen."

"And then Billy Breville got thrown from his horse."

"Ah yes, I saw Billy earlier."

"And we had a man in the pub the other day picking fights with some of my locals. I had to throw him out onto the street and hose him down to cool off!" Barbara added.

Annabelle looked doubtfully at the two women. She was extremely reluctant to pay attention to their gossip but she had to admit she was intrigued by the group of strangers.

"Hmm, well, I'm sure it's all just a coincidence."

"There's no such thing as coincidences, Reverend. No such thing. It's all God's work." Philippa clasped her hands around her knee and leant back, pursing her lips.

"Speaking of God's work, are you seeing the inspector

this week, Reverend?" Barbara asked, her eyes wide, her eyebrows high.

Annabelle wasn't sure what God had to do with the relationship between her and the inspector but she knew the villager's interest in it was intense. Since their return from Scotland some weeks earlier, they had taken to walking their dogs together. They had been seen in all weathers crisscrossing the fields surrounding Upton St. Mary.

The newsagent was keeping a running tab of their sightings. The barman at the Silver Swan was taking bets on an engagement. Meanwhile, a group of twelve-year-olds had lain in wait one Sunday afternoon, vowing to follow the pair throughout their ramble. Possibly because the inspector had been onto them before they'd even left the village, the children had been left for dust at the one-mile mark. Thwarted, they'd gone home to update their parents who pretended to tell them off whilst hanging on to every word.

Annabelle knew all this because she would overhear snippets of gossip. She'd find conversations swiftly concluded when she walked into a room. However, no one, not even Philippa, had dared breathe a word to her directly.

Annabelle took it all in good humour, although she had developed an enormous amount of sympathy for celebrity couples who seemingly had the populations of entire countries hanging on their relationship's every development. The truth in her case was, however, far more mundane.

Although Mike came to the village with Molly every weekend, and their walks across the countryside were the highlight of Annabelle's week, even more so than Sunday communion, their relationship hadn't progressed beyond the occasional hand-holding. She was in quite a tizzy and desperately wanted things to move on, but the inspector appeared to be taking his time. She didn't know what to make of it and was determined to keep everyone in the dark until she did.

She knew her being a vicar may be part of the slow-moving nature of their relationship. If it were, it wouldn't be the first time Annabelle's clerical collar had stood in the way of her love life. She had long ago reconciled herself to the fact that her cassock wasn't exactly an aphrodisiac. This was, in large part, why her long country walks with Inspector Mike Nicholls and their passionate, far-reaching discussions about the state of the world, religion, and the goodness and badness of people from their different perspectives had warmed her heart towards him.

She was sure he enjoyed their time together as much as she did, but she also knew, of course, that in many people's eyes, being a vicar put her in a class of women quite different from the norm. What often people overlooked, however, was that underneath her clerical robes, she was just like any other. She was a girl who wanted love, companionship, and someone she could rely on.

"No, he's gone to a conference," she replied to Barbara, ignoring the older woman's big eyes. "'Innovation and Learning in 21st Century Policing.' He couldn't wait." Annabelle rolled her eyes. Mike hadn't been exactly enthusiastic about the conference. She remembered the words "poncy" and "pointless" being used. "But I'm looking after Molly for him whilst he's away."

Annabelle let out a small sigh, and Barbara leant over to pat her hand. "Don't worry, the time will fly by, dear," she said, her eyes conveying that she knew full well that it wouldn't.

Annabelle sat up straight on the bench. "Oh! It's nothing. I have much too much to be doing. There's a show to put on for starters and many children to corral."

In an instant, Annabelle made a resolution. She would find out more about the strange group living in the house at the end of Lolly Lane. It would distract her from the inspector's absence. She drained her cup. She would keep her plans to herself for the time being.

"I'd better get going. We have a rehearsal at two, and those children won't direct themselves. Thank you for the cupcakes, Philippa." Annabelle leant over. "And the makeup, Barbara."

CHAPTER FOUR

AFTER A BUSY week, the Saturday morning market was once more in full swing. Annabelle wandered from stall to stall, greeting market sellers and customers alike. It made her heart sing to see this centuries-old tradition still running. For many locals, their Saturday morning visits to the market were an important part of their week, the trips carefully planned and executed. Furthermore, buying fresh produce and meeting up with friends on a Saturday morning forced the villagers to rise early rather than idle their time away with a lie-in.

It was barely ten o'clock, but it was already sweltering. The weather had been unseasonably warm over the past few days, and as much as they longed for sunshine when they didn't have it, people were ready for this hot, humid heatwave to be over.

"I'll be in church tomorrow, Reverend. It'll be the coolest place in town," a stout woman of around fifty said, holding out the neck of her low-cut shirt and flapping it vigorously back and forth.

"It's always the coolest place in town, Mrs. Beamish." Annabelle winked.

She waved to the ladies on the WI stall, but skirted it, mindful of the danger it posed to her waistline. She'd been "good" all week, and she didn't want to mess things up now.

Today Annabelle had eschewed her cassock and was wearing a cotton shirt and shorts along with her clerical collar. Whilst her working robes were inordinately forgiving, Annabelle's "civvies" had been getting tighter in recent months. Now though, she could tell her hard work was paying off. Her clothes were feeling a little looser. She reminded herself of the promise she'd made. A shop in London sold "clergy couture," and she'd vowed to treat herself when she'd lost a few pounds.

"Whoops! Sorry!" Annabelle yelped as she stepped back into the path of old Mrs. Penhaligon.

Mrs. Penhaligon was an elderly lady of, rumour had it, around ninety-five. She was a little stooped as she pushed along her wheeled shopping basket, a prized possession donated to her by the church. Annabelle, keen to help keep the elderly independent and connected to the life of the village, had instigated a fundraising drive to deliver these rolling carts to every villager over the age of seventy. The parish council, urged on by Annabelle, had organised bake sales and bingo nights to pay for the carts made in Mr. Carrick's workshop on Poldark Street.

Mr. Carrick, an enthusiastic, amateur metalworker, had volunteered to build the carts. He was a perfectionist, and it hadn't been an easy or inexpensive job, the ageing village population being the size it was. However, the carts had proven to be indestructible. Annabelle was confident they would easily outlive their owners, and she secretly hoped they would be passed down from generation to generation, making them bargains at their price.

"That's okay, dear. No harm done," Mrs. Penhaligon said with a wave.

Annabelle waited as Cynthia Turnbull gave her daughter an arithmetic lesson at Mr. Plumber's fruit and veg stall. "The strawberries are two pounds fifty. If we give him a five-pound note, how much change does Mr. Plumber give us back, Jessica?"

Subtraction was obviously not Jessica's strong point, because, by the time she'd worked out the correct answer, Annabelle was sweating and doing her best to squeeze under the awning of the stall so that she wouldn't melt in the sun.

Finally, Annabelle's turn came around. She chose her vegetables carefully. Mr. Plumber, who was something of a showman, held the brown bag of carrots high and twirled it over on itself. He popped it into Annabelle's bag.

"That'll be seven pounds, eighty, Reverend!"

"Thanks, Mr. Plumber." Annabelle handed him eight pounds, a five-pound note that always reminded her of the toy money she had kept in her play cash register as a child, and three one-pound coins.

As she turned, organising her carrots, and potatoes, and apples, and raspberries so that nothing got squashed in her bag, Annabelle caught sight of the two women she'd seen the previous Saturday. They were dressed as before, the younger one wearing a long, flowing dress, the other wearing clothes suitable for gardening. Cradled against the second woman's chest was the tiny rabbit, its big ears flopping over the back of her hand. They were alone, wandering around the market, chatting quietly.

Annabelle watched them as they stopped to browse a

bric-a-brac stall, the younger, taller woman picking up a pot and turning it over. She said something to the stall owner and pulled out a coin purse, handing over her money and pushing the pot into the fabric bag she carried over her arm. The older woman stood back, stroking the rabbit on her chest, but when a young girl with blonde braids excitedly ran up and reached out to pet the rabbit before rushing away again, she leant down to let her do so.

Annabelle strode up to the two women. "Busy this morning, isn't it? Surprising in this heat," she said cheerily.

The older woman looked at her. She was middle-aged, about fifty, Annabelle guessed. Lines were beginning to crease her face around her eyes and mouth. She had short, cropped hair like a boy, and whilst she stood a good six inches shorter than five-foot-eleven Annabelle, there was a steeliness to her. Veins tracked her forearms where she had rolled back the sleeves of her plaid shirt.

"It is," the woman said. She looked away from Annabelle and back to her companion, who was completing her transaction.

Annabelle tried again. "I'm Annabelle Dixon, the local vicar, the reverend at St. Mary's." She pointed to the spire of the five-hundred-year-old church, a beacon noticeable from anywhere in the village.

"Cool," the woman said, her eyes still focused on her friend.

"You're new here, I believe. Don't you live in the big house at the end of Lolly Lane?"

"Yes, that's right. We moved in about three weeks ago." The woman glanced at Annabelle but looked away when her friend turned to join them.

Annabelle smiled at the younger woman and stuck out her hand. "Hello, I'm Reverend Annabelle Dixon, the local vicar. I'd like to welcome you to Upton St. Mary. You are . . . ?"

The woman took her hand lightly. "Sally. Sally Venables. This is my friend, Julia Snow. Yes, we moved in recently. We're loving it here so far. Such a friendly community, and the countryside's just beautiful."

"Can I stand you for a cup of tea? Best thing to cool you down on a hot day, don't you think? And perhaps a drink for your, um, little friend there?" Annabelle nodded at the rabbit who's nose was twitching, its intense, dark eyes blinking in the sun. "I always like to get to know newcomers to the village, and all this shopping is thirsty work."

"We'd love that, wouldn't we, Julia?"

Julia shrugged but followed her friend. Together, they crossed the road to Flynn's and found an empty table at the back. The tea shop was quieter this week.

As they waited for their tea to arrive, Annabelle reached out a hand and ran a finger between the rabbit's ears. Its fur was silky, velvety, and smooth.

"I used to have rabbits when I was a girl," Annabelle told Julia. "I loved my dwarf lops. Such soft fur and those ears are so cute."

Julia sat up a little straighter, surprised by this revelation. She leant forwards, her gaze relaxing. "Would you like to hold him?" She handed the small rabbit to Annabelle, who cradled it in the crook of her arm. She ran her other hand over its back.

A couple came into the tearoom. They looked at Annabelle curiously, but she took no notice. Rabbits were God's creatures, after all. Holding her teacup with her free hand, taking a sip, and turning to look at Sally, Annabelle asked, "So where have you moved from?"

Annabelle guessed Sally to be in her early twenties. She

was tall enough to be elegant without being so tall that she was awkward. Annabelle regarded her ruefully. A small, delicately curved nose, blue, sparkling eyes, and an easy smile turned the heads of even the female patrons of the tea shop. Sally's loose, flowing dress couldn't hide her tiny waist. She had long, slender limbs and shoulder-length, wavy blonde hair. She was pretty much the kind of woman Annabelle imagined herself to be in her dreams.

"We moved from up north. We'd been there for six months, and it was time to move on. We like to move about, but I think the brotherhood will stay put for a while now we're here," Sally said.

"Brotherhood?" Annabelle gulped her tea a little too fast and choked.

"We're members of the Brotherhood of St. Petrie. You've probably heard of him, you being a vicar and all."

"No," Annabelle said slowly, frowning. "Can't say that I have." She frantically searched her brain for a memory that would help her. "Perhaps he was one of the minor saints."

"Well, anyway, we live very simply. Sustainable, vegan living. We help the communities we live among. We meditate a lot, and do our very best to live our lives for the highest good."

"I see, and how many of you are there?" Annabelle asked. Sally looked up at the ceiling, counting in her head.

"Five, officially." Julia cut in. Her face was stern, and she fiddled with her teaspoon. "Two more, unofficially," she added, her voice low, almost a growl.

Sally said, "There's me and Julia. Theo, of course, he's our leader, Scott, and Thomas. Theo's sister, Suki, and his mother, Margaret, also live with us, but they're not members, not officially. They just tag along."

Julia took a sip of her tea. Annabelle couldn't discern

whether the grimace that formed as Julia replaced her cup in its saucer was due to the strength of her tea or her opinion of the two hangers-on.

"Hmm, and how are you getting along, in the village, *with* the villagers?"

"They're very nice, in the main," Sally said. "They're a little distant, understandably. We can take some getting used to, what with our ways, but we rub along quite well, wouldn't you say, Julia?" Julia gave a curt nod.

"Do you get any trouble? Heckling or hostility?"

"Sometimes, but there's no need. We don't mean any harm. Why? Have you had any complaints?" A small frown creased Sally's pale, smooth forehead.

"Well, you see, you seem very straightforward sorts, but the thing is, the villagers are rather disturbed. You talk to people, people you don't know, and hand out flowers. We're not used to that kind of thing here. The villagers are a little frightened of you, I think. They get a little suspicious. They wonder what you're after."

"We just want to be welcoming and friendly, Reverend. We share our beliefs, and if anyone's interested, they can visit us to find out more, but there's no pressure."

Annabelle placed her cup carefully in her saucer. She wiped the fingertips of one hand on her napkin, the other still holding the rabbit. "Let me speak more plainly. People believe you to be a cult. That conjures up thoughts of strangeness, weirdness, brainwashing, ritual sacrifices, even evil."

"Oh, we're not like that at all!" Julia said. She sat forwards in her chair and reached over to take the rabbit. At the sound of Julia's voice, the animal had quickly travelled from the crook of Annabelle's arm to her shoulder. It was now nibbling her ear. "We love our animals, don't we, Barnaby?" she crooned, picking him up and going nose to nose with the bunny. "There's no ritualistic killings or evil goings-on at all. I wouldn't allow it, not around the animals. Whilst you and I are mere imperfect beings, Reverend, animals embody all that is kind and good in the world. They represent the highest form of living. We humans can only hope to live up to their ideal."

"What Julia means is that we love all living creatures equally. We believe good works are rewarded in the next life and so endeavour to do as many as we can as we live this one. We hope to recruit others to our mission and in so doing, lighten their souls," Sally said. Annabelle looked from one woman to the other, a shadow of doubt crossing her brow.

"Look, if you don't believe us, why don't you visit? Come and meet us all. How about the day after tomorrow? Theo will be back from London. He can tell you all about us. He'll reassure you, and maybe then you can reassure the village."

Annabelle considered the idea for a moment. Competing voices shouted loudly in her head. On the one hand, she felt there was something not quite on the up and up about the group. She hated the idea that her presence would give them credence, even acceptability. But her curiosity and the need for distraction argued for accepting Sally's invitation. Maybe, just maybe, the group would turn out to be as benign as the two women next to her insisted.

"Alright," she said. "I accept your invitation. Thank you."

"Marvellous," Sally said, draining her cup. "How about five on Monday?"

"Perfect."

They stood to leave. Julia popped Barnaby into her

pocket. "No need to dress up, we're quite casual. We'll look forward to seeing you, Reverend," she said, much more friendly now.

"Goodbye, Julia, Sally, er . . ." Annabelle looked down. "Barnaby." The bunny's button nose bobbed back at her.

CHAPTER FIVE

ANNABELLE DECIDED TO park her car in Lolly Lane and walk the rest of the way. The path comprised an ancient dirt track left to form naturally from rocks, stones, and sandy soil beaten down over centuries by herds of animals on their way to grazing pasture. At intervals, the track was dotted with potholes. In rainy weather, they were the size of small ponds but currently resembled craters on the moon's surface.

In her hands, Annabelle carefully carried a rhubarb flan, a gift for her hosts. She tip-toed along the straight track that led up a slight incline, walking in a zig-zag pattern as she avoided obstacles that lay across her path. Bramble had grown over the Cornish stone walls that separated the lane from the fields on either side. Grasses, cow parsley, and the occasional crop of daisies or wild pink betony made up the hedgerow and grassy margins.

As she aimed for the iron gate that marked the border of the estate on which the Brotherhood of St. Petrie lived, Annabelle passed Mr. and Mrs. Cuddy's home, Oakcombe Cottage. Their front garden frothed with wildflowers in full bloom. Stems of navelwort, their red trunks supporting masses of tiny, ground-pointing, pale green tubes, stood tall and majestic in deep flowerbeds. Whenever she saw navelwort, Annabelle imagined hundreds of tiny trumpets ready to announce the arrival of a fairy army. Her thought always made her walk a little more carefully. Lower to the ground, poppies, wild honeysuckle, and buttercups flourished.

The Cuddy's adored their garden but admitted that their green fingers stretched only as far as allowing the plants to self-germinate and granting whatever wildlife that found its way to their "little patch of heaven" a free roam. The cottage's owners regularly spotted birds, bees, butterflies, hedgehogs, and even a family of badgers among their flowers and shrubs. "We believe in letting nature do its thing," Mr. Cuddy had once told Annabelle. "We can't take any credit."

It was a hot afternoon, and the atmosphere continued to be muggy. Nonetheless, Annabelle marched on, banishing the thought of fairy armies and foraging animals from her mind. She passed the other house on Lolly Lane and paused to dab her brow. The Hamiltons lived here. They were a family of five, but their garden was as much a study in order as the Cuddy's was in chaos.

A neat, bright green lawn spread from the front of the house to the back. There was a swing set off to one side, and bikes propped up against the wall of a large, wooden shed that served as a garage. Flowerbeds filled with white rosebushes, pruned with care for symmetry and balance, graced one corner of their patch of land whilst a royal blue front door brightened up the rather dour, grey, boxy, brick house that served as the Hamilton's home.

The house lacked the charm of the Cuddy's cottage, which looked as if it was lifted from a picture postcard with its thatched roof, cream exterior, and small leaded windows. But the two eldest Hamilton girls, Eleanor and Elaine, were senior cast members in Annabelle's show and she knew them to be a kind and happy family with good manners and a border collie named "Lass." There was no sign of anyone home.

Annabelle cruised by, panting and sweating a little from the long walk and the heat before she finally came to a five-bar gate. She lifted the metal catch and pushed it open with a shove, brushing aside the bracken that held it fast. Once free, it swung open with a long creak, and she passed into the wooded area beyond.

It wasn't unusual in these parts to have a large house surrounded by trees, but as she closed the gate behind her, Annabelle slowed her pace. She looked above her, wide-eyed. The trees grew close together, and the mass of leaves high above formed a canopy that made the area very dark. At least it was blessedly cool.

Bending her head and looking where she placed her feet, Annabelle pressed on. It was nearly five o'clock, and she hoped Sally and Julia would be waiting for her. Annabelle had told no one she was making this visit, certainly not Philippa, who she suspected would have been horrified.

Eventually, the trees came to an end. Annabelle emerged onto a lawn bisected by a path leading up to the large house. Annabelle stopped to stare at it. She hadn't visited before. It had clearly been magnificent in its heyday, and even though it was now crumbling and in need of restoration, Annabelle could still detect hints of the stately majesty the house had once embodied.

The house resembled a mini castle. Rounded turrets propped up the outside walls at each corner. It was built with traditional Cornish red stone with tall windows running in two rows on all the sides that Annabelle could see. She imagined those who lived there looking out at the stunning views—vast, sweeping lawns, imposing, centuries-old trees, dense woodland, and rolling, pillow-like hills.

From where she stood, Annabelle could picture what the house must have looked like in its prime. Now though, it was looking a little tired and worn. Some of the crenellations at the top of the turrets were missing, the stonework chipped and disintegrating in places. The hydrangea bushes dotted around the house were wild and straggly, whilst the boxwoods that guarded the path to the huge front double doors were stringy and misshapen. Annabelle could just make out the rounded, inverted, pyramid shapes topiarists had clipped into them in times past.

Annabelle was tired now and regretted her decision to leave her Mini in Lolly Lane. She trudged her way to the double front door, clambering up the wide, stone steps. She knocked on it a little breathlessly. No one came, so Annabelle tried again, the flat of her hand painful as she slapped the flaking, splintering wood. Still, no one arrived to welcome her. She tried the handle. The door opened, creaking as it swung wide.

"Hello? Cooee? Anyone home?" she called out, peering inside. She tentatively took a step over the threshold and looked around.

Annabelle's heels clacked as she walked across the stone floor, her voice echoing, reverberating around the low-lit cavernous entrance hall. Enormous stairs opened up in front of her. The air was musty, there was a stale patina of age, dampness, and neglect to it. On the ground floor, doors leading to other parts of the house were closed, the paint on the walls peeling and cracked. Dust cloths lay over furniture like strangely shaped body bags, dirty and faded. Annabelle peered through the gloom, looking for signs of life.

Spying a door on the other side of the vestibule, Annabelle took a deep breath and walked over to it. The glass in the paned door was filthy with dust and age. She cleared it with her fingertips. Annabelle placed her eye close enough to peer through the glass and spied a courtyard which, due to a lack of care and the passage of time, was now more yard than court. Piles of bird droppings punctuated the ground. Weeds grew up between the cracked, uneven paving. Elaborate stone planters shaped like tulip heads stood broken and empty. The courtyard was only saved from an air of complete decrepitude by the open sky and the caw of circling seagulls.

Annabelle heard a low rumble of voices. She looked over, and at the end of the sunny courtyard saw a woman lounging in a wooden deck chair, the kind of which Annabelle avoided. She couldn't work them without pinching her fingers. The woman was smoking a long, thin cigarette, her skin prematurely aged by the habit and the sun that she was soaking up. The woman was talking to Sally, who was perched on a cushion atop an upturned flowerpot, shelling peas into a bowl.

Annabelle tried the door handle. "Cooee! Sally!" she waved as the door opened. Sally looked up.

"Reverend! You made it!" Sally put down her bowl of peas and stood, brushing her skirts. "It's lovely to see you. Come here!" She walked over to Annabelle and gave her a hug. Annabelle offered her the rhubarb flan. "Oh, thank you!" Sally cried. "Come and meet Margaret. I've been telling her about you." She took Annabelle's hand, her long, full skirt billowing around her. Annabelle allowed herself to be taken over to the woman in the deckchair, who made no move to get up or put out her cigarette.

"Margaret, this is Reverend Dixon from the church in the village. Remember, I told you she was visiting today?" Margaret didn't appear to recollect anything of the sort but, still sitting, she held her hand out for Annabelle to grasp. "Annabelle, this is Margaret Westmoreland."

"Pleased to meet you, Reverend," Margaret said, not smiling or indicating pleasure of any kind. Margaret's hooded eyes were a little too close together, her nose too broad, and her mouth too small, but there was a symmetry to her face and an intelligence that marked her as attractive, if rather dispassionate. Her short, wavy hair was styled in a fashion more suited to the sixties, whilst her slim frame was draped in a grey and cream cotton sundress that reached her ankles. She wore flat, brown, strappy sandals. Her toenails were painted a Pepto-Bismol pink. Tiny studs made from seashells of a far more delicate pinkish shade graced her ears.

"Likewise, Ms. Westmoreland," Annabelle responded, eyeing the woman carefully. She refused to compensate for the woman's imperiousness by being overly enthusiastic. She thought it better, on this occasion, to be measured and calm until she got the lie of this suspected "cult."

"Please, call me Margaret," the woman said. "And what should I call you?" Margaret lazily looked up at Annabelle. A wisp of smoke escaped her lips. She sucked it back in again, smiling slowly.

"Oh, Reverend should do it, I'd say," Annabelle replied cheerily, unwilling to give this superior woman the opportunity to patronise her. As Margaret Westmoreland's smile vanished, the older woman's gaze hardened. "Or Vicar. That works too," Annabelle added.

Margaret lowered her lids and regarded Annabelle. "I think I'll leave you ladies to it," she said, suddenly stabbing her cigarette into the ashtray on the steps next to her. "Help me up, would you, Sally?" Sally grabbed the older woman's hand and pulled her up. Margaret straightened her dress and walked into the house. "I'll be in my room if you need me. Goodbye, *Reverend.*"

Sally looked at Annabelle and grimaced. "Sorry about that. Margaret is Theo's mother. She's not part of the brotherhood. She just lives here with us. She can be a little, hmmm, *difficult* at times."

"No problem, Sally. I understand." Annabelle surveyed the courtyard and the four walls that surrounded it. "Tell me, this is a lovely house, at least it was once. How did you come to be here?"

"Honestly, Reverend, I don't know the full story. It's owned by someone in Theo's family, I believe. It's too big for us really. We live mostly in this part of the house, the old servant's quarters, although our bedrooms are spread all over. It suits us. Come on in, we'll be having dinner soon. Would you like to stay and eat with us?"

CHAPTER SIX

ANNABELLE AND SALLY moved to the kitchen. It was a big square room with green cupboards and a white tile backsplash around the edges. The green paint on the cupboard doors was flaking. The grout between the tiles, grey with age, was missing in places. Under the window lay a large, deep, rectangular porcelain sink.

In the middle of the room sat an enormous wooden table. Julia was sitting at it, peeling carrots. Barnaby was on the table eating the green tops.

"Hello again, Reverend," Julia said. "Joining us for dinner? We've got soup with homemade bread made by yours truly, coconut curry with quinoa, and crumble for afters."

"That sounds tasty," Annabelle replied.

"It's quite a feast because we're celebrating."

"Oh?"

"Tonight we celebrate the legend of St. Petrie and Lord Darthamort," Sally explained.

"And how do you do that?" Annabelle asked. She sat

down at the table and stroked Barnaby's soft, soft fur as he nibbled.

"We have a big bonfire, dance around like mad things, and make a lot of noise," Sally said. "It's fun."

The door to the kitchen opened and in poured another young woman, impossibly beautiful and willowy. She, like Sally, wore a long flowing dress, although she carried herself more sensually. The dress's short, puffed sleeves were pushed off her shoulders, the neckline low on her chest. Her blonde hair was pinned up in a messy do, tendrils falling around her face and onto her shoulders. Long droplets of gold dangled from her ears.

"Sally, darling, could you put this on for me?" The woman walked up to Sally and turned her back. In her hand was a tiny weaved chain of gold. Sally took it from her and dutifully draped the necklace around the other woman's throat, linking one end inside the clasp.

"There, all done," Sally said, patting the woman's shoulder lightly.

"Thank you, darling." The woman spun around and caught sight of Annabelle. "Oh!"

"Suki, this is the vicar of St. Mary's in the village. She's come to visit us and see what we're about."

Suki rolled her eyes. "Well, that's exciting! We're quite the party animals here, you know. It's just non-stop fun *all* the time." She eyed Annabelle's clerical collar. "I'm sure you'll feel quite at home."

Annabelle looked at her, unsure what to make of this exotic creature. The run-down kitchen was hardly her natural habitat.

"This is Suki, Reverend. Theo's sister," Sally said.

"Are you having dinner with us tonight, Suki?" Julia asked.

"Oh, I suppose so, if I must."

"And will you join us for the celebration afterwards?"

"Oh God, is that tonight? Will Theo be terribly angry if I say no?"

"You know he will."

Suki sighed. "But it's all such a bore. All that yelling and galumphing about is so unladylike."

"It's cleansing for the soul, Suki," Julia said. "You should try it sometime." Julia was attacking the carrots, peeling more off than she was leaving behind. Still, more for Barnaby.

"The only cleansing I'm interested in, Julia, is the kind one gets at a spa."

Julia tutted and blew out her cheeks. She focused on her carrots with a fury of scraping.

"You know Theo hates it when you don't join in, Suki," Sally said. "We'll all be there. It won't be as much fun if you're not."

Suki draped an arm around Sally's neck and regarded her before seeming to come to a decision. She kissed Sally's cheek. "Well, alright then. For you, darling." Suki turned to Annabelle. "Will you be there, Reverend?"

"Um . . ."

"You really should come see how the other half lives." Suki eyed Annabelle's clerical collar again and laughed. It sounded like the pealing of bells rung after Sunday service; the rapid, light, tinkling sounds mirroring the feelings of the parishioners who, their weekly worship seen to and the difficulties of the prior week dispensed with, felt cleansed and re-energised, ready for the seven days ahead.

"We're meeting for dinner at seven, and we'll get ready for the celebration at eight," Sally said.

Suki gave a melodramatic sigh. "Oh well, seeing as

there's no alternative, I shall go and prepare myself." She made big eyes at Annabelle and picked up her skirts. "I'm off to have a pre-dinner drink." With that, Suki spun, flapping her skirts with a flourish of a flamenco dancer. She strode off.

"That girl," Julia grumbled.

"Leave her alone, Julia," Sally admonished. "It can't be easy for her living here. Not after what she's used to."

"My heart bleeds."

"Suki's father was a banker in London," Sally explained. "Lost all his money in the crash, then died of a heart attack. Margaret and Suki are forced to live here with us."

"No, they're not, Sally," Julia said. "They could get jobs just like anyone else. They're not *forced* to do anything. They don't even contribute to the food kitty."

"How do you support yourselves here?" Annabelle asked.

"We live simply, so we don't need too much," Sally said. "We pay a peppercorn rent for this house thanks to Theo's family connections. We pool our money and share all the bills and food. Nothing goes to waste. We make money by selling the things that we produce. We make jam in season and sell that along with our chutneys."

Julia pointed outside with her peeler. "We grow vegetables, and we knit. One of our group is a smithy and a farrier. We sell metalwork items that he makes. Another of our members is a photographer. He turns his photos into cards and calendars, those kinds of things. Money can get a bit tight at times, especially in the winter, but we manage."

"We do ask for donations now and again, but we always give something in return, flowers or blessings. And then there's our newsletter, *The Petrie Dish*," Sally said proudly. "That's Theo's baby. We make a bit from that."

"We could do more," Julia said, her mouth downturned. Barnaby, now sufficiently replete, was starting to hop around the table, his velvety ears dusting the surface. "We have this huge place, loads of land, and we have no plans to do anything with it. It's just going to waste."

"Julia, you know what Theo said. It wasn't feasible. How would we feed all the animals?" Sally turned to Annabelle. "Julia wants to open an animal sanctuary, but Theo shot down the idea. He said it would be too costly to set up."

"What he actually *said* was that we could set up an animal sanctuary *over his dead body*. Theo is a self-entitled, self-indulgent—"

"Julia, stop it. Your plans were so grand."

"It was just a simple donkey sanctuary! A few donkeys! And maybe some moor ponies. Do you know how terrible their life is? There isn't enough food for them in the wild. Some of them are starving to death!" Julia protested. "But of course, Theo could see no use for them and thought they would be a liability and a waste of time."

The sound of boots bounding up the steps outside reached them. The door opened with a bang.

"Evening, ladies."

Annabelle turned to see a young, lithe man cross the threshold. He shared the same colouring as Suki, there was a distinct family resemblance. But where Suki possessed a world-weary insouciance, her brother had an easy smile and lively, twinkling eyes. He was dressed casually in a button-down shirt, sleeves rolled up to his elbows, and faded jeans. He had scuffed cowboy boots on his feet.

Sally beamed when she saw him. She bounded over.

"*This* is Theo!" She put her arm around his shoulders. The young man looked at Annabelle as he swung his arm proprietorially around Sally's waist. "Hello."

"Theo, this is Reverend Annabelle Dixon from Upton St. Mary, the village down the road. She's come to meet us."

Annabelle stood. Theo's eyes widened, and he held her gaze. He took her hand and bent over, raising her fingers to his lips.

"Charmed, Reverend," he murmured, capturing her again with a direct look as he stood upright.

"Oh, um, nice to meet you, Theo. I thought I'd pay you a visit and welcome you to the area, introduce myself." Theo was certainly dashing, and Annabelle felt herself becoming self-conscious under his gaze. Her face flushed a little.

"You've certainly chosen a wild night to visit us."

"Have I?"

"Haven't the girls told you? Tonight is the night we celebrate the legend of St. Petrie and Lord Darthamort."

"Ah yes, they did mention it. Perhaps you could tell me more about this St. Petrie. I can't say I've heard of him."

"You haven't heard of the legend of St. Petrie and Lord Darthamort?" Theo let go of Sally and pulled out a chair. Annabelle shifted slightly away from him, expecting him to sit next to her, but Theo put his foot on the seat and leant on his knee, supporting himself on his forearm. His hand dangled level with her chin, and Annabelle noticed a small, faded tattoo in the crease between his thumb and forefinger. It was a swastika.

Theo looked down at her. "Legend has it that St. Petrie and his companion, Lord Darthamort, work together to reward the good and punish the bad. Darthamort is a half-goat, half-demon figure that punishes criminals and other

unpleasant people, whilst St. Petrie, a benevolent soul manifested in human form, rewards the good with gold. It's a
legend that originated in Bavaria circa 1534. A movement
grew up in the early part of the twentieth century that advo-
cated vigilante justice in areas where law enforcement was
considered inadequate or non-existent. The legend was
adopted as their rallying point, the message as a manifesto,
and the Darthamort and St. Petrie characters as mascots.
The movement gained momentum in Europe but faded
away as Hitler came to power."

"Oh my, that sounds rather sinister." Annabelle was
taken aback.

"Oh, not at all. Today, nothing like a movement exists,
of course, but still in Northern Europe, the legend is cele-
brated with parades and the Darthamortlauf."

"The what?"

"It means the Darthamort run. Young men dressed as
Lord Darthamort run through crowds with tiki torches,
cracking whips and scaring small children. It takes place
mostly in towns in Germany, Austria, and Switzerland. It's
all a bit of fun, really."

"It doesn't sound like it."

"Oh, the crowds only pretend to be scared. They love it,
really."

"But how does this relate to you here? We have no such
traditions." *Thank goodness.* "Why do you celebrate the
legend?"

"The idea of rewarding good whilst punishing evil is
universal, I think we can all agree on that. We don't go in for
all that vigilante nonsense, but here at the brotherhood, we
like to perform good deeds and hope to spread good cheer.
We stand against evil when we encounter it. Twice a year
we have our own version of the Darthamort run. We'll be

doing it tonight, in fact, after dinner. Are you staying for dinner?"

"Oh, I don't know." Annabelle looked about her, flustered.

"Please do, Reverend, we'd love to have you," Sally said.

"Certainly we would. The more the merrier, especially this evening," Theo said. "Have you been given the grand tour yet?"

"No, no, I haven't."

Theo looked at Julia and Sally. "Well, let's leave the girls to work." Julia let out a low growl. "And allow me the honour of showing you around the old house. Dinner should be ready in . . . ?" Theo looked quizzically at Sally.

"About an hour or so."

"Perfect." Theo held out his arm for Annabelle to take and despite her reservations, she found herself swept away by this charming, handsome, charismatic man.

CHAPTER SEVEN

THEY SAT IN a cluttered room in the main part of the house. The huge, arched, leaded window at one end framed the early evening summer sun streaming into the room, exaggerating the dirt and dust caked on the glass. It bathed them in a warm, hazy glow.

Around the table sat Annabelle and the group members she had met earlier, Sally, Julia, Suki, and Theo. Two other members of the brotherhood had joined them and were introduced to Annabelle as Thomas and Scott. Margaret was missing. No one mentioned her.

Theo sat at the end of the large oval table in front of the window. He was cast in shadow, the sun behind him creating a golden aura around his silhouette like an enormous halo. Suki and Sally sat on either side of him. Scott and Thomas, who Annabelle recognised as the men she had seen at the market, still had their tiny plaited ponytails, but their knickerbockers had been replaced by chinos. Annabelle sat between them.

Theo raised his arms to say grace. As she observed the scene, it struck Annabelle that it looked like a cross between the Last Supper and the Resurrection. The group held hands and closed their eyes, but Annabelle kept hers wide open. Suki caught her eye and winked.

"Let's praise St. Petrie for blessing us with this food." It was a grace unlike any Annabelle had ever heard. "Thank you for meeting our physical needs of hunger and thirst. We praise you for the bounty that you provide. Bless this food as we fuel our bodies and souls so that we may work for the glory of your name. Bless us, the family and friends beside us, and the love we share." Theo opened his eyes. "Amen. Let us eat."

"It may look like the River Thames after a bad storm, but it's actually a vegan soup," Suki reassured Annabelle as she passed her a bowl of thick, grey slurry. "It's full of good-ness. And quite tasty if you're hungry." She leant in to whis-per. "Best of all, it has virtually no calories."

A salad of rocket leaves and kale topped with orange, red, and green heritage tomatoes lay in a wooden bowl on the table alongside a tray of dense, rustic bread. "All the results of our own efforts. The hot weather ripened the tomatoes early this year," Julia told Annabelle, her eyes sparkling.

The soup was surprisingly good and extremely filling. Annabelle chatted to Thomas and Scott on either side of her. "And what do you do, Thomas?"

"Er, I-I'm a photographer."

Thomas sat silently, his chair set back from the table a little, one pudgy hand placed on his knee as he supported himself, the sleeves of his button-down shirt rolled up to his elbows. There was a slight sheen on his forehead and he repeatedly pushed his round, rimless glasses higher on his nose whilst avoiding virtually all eye contact with those around him. His wispy, pale hair was damp from the warm summer evening. He ran a fingertip across his brow.

"What kind of photography do you do?"

"Ohh, m–mostly nature. I enjoy roaming the country-side and taking pictures of the animals, the landscape, drops of dew on a leaf, that k-kind of thing." He paused and glanced at Annabelle before continuing, "but I do take typical C-Cornish shots, like the fishing boats and c–cream teas." He paused again. "They're especially popular with the tourists. I sell a lot of postcards of s–scones, j–jam, and," Thomas gathered himself to put extra effort into his final words, "clotted cream."

"And how long have you been with the brotherhood? I hear you moved down from the north a short while ago."

"A couple of years." Thomas' confidence increased as he spoke. Annabelle's interested expression never strayed from his face. He sat up straighter, taking his eyes off his soup to flick glances at her as he spoke. "Ever since my mother went into a h–home." Thomas finished his sentence with a whisper. "She's in her eighties," he said, trailing off.

"I hope she's happy there."

"I lived with her until I could n–no longer care for her." Thomas looked down at his lap, but sensing that he had a sympathetic listener, lifted his gaze quickly. "We had to sell her house to pay for the home. I was living hand to mouth for a while. Then I bumped into Theo one day whilst I was out taking pictures, and he offered me a place to stay. He was very kind."

Thomas pulled a photograph from his pocket. It was of a falcon with a smaller bird caught between its claws. "S–sorry for the s–strong subject matter, V-vicar. It was such a s–stunning s–sight. The falcon just s–swooped down and s–scooped the other bird up."

"It is remarkable, isn't it? Nature can be brutal, I see it all the time." Annabelle thought back to the children at the most recent rehearsal. "All part of God's holy plan, I suppose. But I have to say, I much prefer pictures of scones and jam and clotted cream. Much more my kind of thing."

She smiled at Thomas, who nodded vigorously and again pushed his glasses higher on his nose. He took a sip of his soup, and the lenses clouded along the lower rim. He looked at her over the fog.

"I like to do things the old-fashioned way. T–trays of developing fluid, stop baths, drying lines, that k–kind of thing. I develop my p–pictures in a room in the east wing. It's very kind of Theo to allow me the space to do that."

"But you contribute to the income of the group, do you not?"

"Well, yes, my p–postcards and greeting c–cards bring in a bit at the local markets, and I occasionally sell large, f–framed p–prints of my wildlife pictures for a decent price."

"Well then, you deserve your space. You've earned it."

Thomas considered Annabelle's point seemingly for the first time. He tucked in his chin. "Perhaps I do," he said, putting a hunk of bread into his mouth and tearing off a big bite.

"And what about you, Scott? What's your story? Where do you come from?" Annabelle turned to the big man on the other side of her. Between his eyes were frown lines that gave him a dark, surly expression, and as he sat hunched over the table, a thick, hairy arm stabbed at his food like he was murdering it. Annabelle thought his behaviour unnecessarily violent considering the meal consisted entirely of plants.

Scott was a blacksmith, and as Annabelle watched him forcefully skewer a misshapen slice of tomato, she questioned the wisdom of his choice of vocation. He didn't seem the sort of person with whom one would want to hang around, especially if he was wielding a red hot poker in one hand and a hammer in the other.

Before Scott answered her, he picked up his soup bowl with bucket-like, red, scarred hands and drank directly from it. Annabelle waited good-naturedly as he drained his bowl and put it down with a bang, smacking his lips together and wiping his mouth with the back of his hand. Out of the corner of her eye, Annabelle saw Suki looking over at Scott with appreciation at what was obviously, in her opinion, clear evidence of testosterone-fuelled masculinity.

"Not much to tell, Vicar. I'm a traveller by heritage, but my parents tired of the life before I was born. I grew up on a rough estate in East Anglia. I think it's in the bones though, travelling, not wanting to stay in one place. I was in regular work, but Theo came up to me one day at a market in Suffolk and asked if I'd like to join the brotherhood. I took a bit of persuading but eventually, it seemed like a good idea. I thought that perhaps it'd be a way to see a bit of the country. I've been with them ever since.

"Do you all get along? I mean, with each other?"

"We can get on each other's nerves at times but we rub along pretty well."

Suki was still staring at Scott. He caught her eye, and barely suppressing an eye roll, he turned his head to Annabelle and pointed to her clerical collar.

"Never been much of a churchgoer meself. What are you doing here?"

"Oh, I'm just checking you out," Annabelle said, widening her eyes. She waggled her head, a smirk flitting across her lips. "Make sure you're on the up and up. Just kidding," she added quickly, when she saw Scott's coarse, meaty hands clench and his expression darken. She wondered if there was a bit more than family history behind Scott's decision to take to the road. "I saw Julia and Sally at the market and thought I'd introduce myself. They invited me here to meet you all. Make sure you're not up to no good." She trilled nervously and thumped her fist on her thigh. Scott regarded her curiously, his frown lines deepening.

"I think you'll find us all just yer ordinary folk, keeping themselves to themselves, if you know what I mean."

"Ah, I know exactly what you mean, Scott," Annabelle agreed. "More salad?"

"Yes, please!" Scott said, his eyes lighting up. "I love a good salad."

"I thought you'd be more of a meat man."

"I was until I got here." Scott tipped up the bowl to scoop the last of the salad onto his plate. "Totally changed what I eat. My diet used to be all meat, preferably wrapped in pastry and washed down with beer. And now here we are in Cornwall, home of the famous Cornish pasty, and I wouldn't touch one of 'em with a barge pole. I love my veg. If she could see me now, my old Ma would be as proud as punch and totally confused, 'cuz I couldn't stand veg when I was a nipper. I wouldn't mind the odd bit of cheese now and again, though."

Scott didn't say any more. Annabelle watched him as she ate Julia's tasty coconut curry. She marvelled at the odd sight of this beefy, hirsute man shovelling lettuce and tomatoes into his mouth, chomping away, his eyes closed in delirium until the clanging of a spoon against a mug interrupted her. Theo stood and waited until he had everyone's attention.

"Peace everyone." He addressed the group as Sally

handed out glasses filled with light gold wine. He cast his eyes around. "As you all know, tonight is the celebration of the legend of our saviours, St. Petrie and Lord Darthamort. I hope you are ready for a fabulous evening. The celebration will commence at nine p.m. sharp down by the bonfire." Theo looked at Annabelle. "I do hope you will join us, Reverend."

Annabelle raised her eyebrows, surprised by this invitation. She looked around the table and saw that all eyes were on her awaiting her answer.

CHAPTER EIGHT

THE OTHERS BANGED the table in a rhythmic, steady beat. Thomas slapped his knee. Scott stamped his foot so hard, the plates bounced on the table. Suki picked up her fork and tapped it against her mug. Even Julia drummed her fingertips on the tabletop.

The beat got faster and faster until there was a cacophony of thumps and bangs as her fellow diners abandoned their rhythm and pounded randomly with their implements. Annabelle put her hands over her ears.

Theo stood like a conductor in front of them, his hands aloft, his eyes closed. Drawing his hands together and then quickly apart with a flourish, he gave the command to end the display, and immediately, everyone went quiet.

Annabelle let out a big sigh of relief. The others at the table looked past her, and she turned to see Sally walk in with the biggest crumble she'd ever seen. It dwarfed her rhubarb flan. She leant over to Thomas and whispered, "What's going on?"

"Th-Theo's just psyching us up for the celebration. He likes them loud. N-None of us are loud people, if you know what I mean, so he revs us up a bit. Gives us some alcohol to help things along, which of course, because we're usually teetotal, has an immediate effect."

"But what's going to happen?"

"After we've had our crumble, we're going to rumble, as we say. We'll go back to our rooms to prepare and then meet outside by the bonfire. Theo will have his "come to Jesus" moment, and then we'll make some noise and dance around a bit. We'll watch the fire burn out and go to bed around midnight. It's just a bit of harmless fun."

Annabelle looked at the other six people around the table. Sally was dishing out the crumble, and they were passing around the bowls. She noticed Julia reach out and spoon cream onto her pudding.

"What's that?" she asked Thomas.

"Pureed tofu. It's not that bad. Go on, have some. It tastes like sour cream."

"Don't you want your crumble, Vicar?" Scott asked her, eyeing her bowl greedily.

"No, no, thank you. I'm being . . . good," Annabelle replied, not looking at him. She was distracted.

"Mind if I have it?" he asked.

"No, go ahead."

Scott pushed his bowl out of the way and slid Annabelle's over to him. He fell upon it greedily. Annabelle barely noticed. She was more concerned with the febrile atmosphere that now pervaded the room and everyone around the table. Gone was the quiet murmur of gentle chitchat, and in its place, the sounds of laughter, shouts, and the odd backslap filled the air. Suki and Sally were arm wrestling. Julia was smiling and jiggling her knees up and down. Thomas was attacking his dessert and letting out loud murmurs of appreciation. Scott finished Annabelle's dessert and began singing to himself whilst performing a strange dance that looked like a mashup of the funky chicken and the macarena. They all appeared giddy with anticipation. Annabelle would have thought them roaring drunk, except they'd only drunk one glass of wine. There was an air of mania present. Cutting through it all, Theo sat watching her serenely. *What had she got herself into?*

There was a bang from the hallway outside. "Hey! *Hey!* Where is she? Sally!" yelled a man.

The raucous scene quietened immediately. Sally went pale and stood up. As she did so, the door burst open, and in came a man, red-faced, unshaven, and rough. He was panting and sweating, wearing an old T-shirt and worn jeans. There were dark shadows under his eyes.

"Sally!"

"Dad, what are you doing here?"

"I've come to get you."

"What? No . . ."

"You're coming home. With me."

"Dad, I—"

The man strode quickly across the room towards his daughter, his jaw and fists clenched tightly. Theo stood gracefully and put himself between the man and Sally, his hands raised.

"Look, Richard—"

"Get out of my way, you." Richard Venables put his hands on Theo's arm to push him. Theo stood firm.

"As I've said to you before, you need to listen to your daughter, Richard."

Venables thrust his red, lined face into Theo's smooth, handsome one. "I've *been* listening. I've listened and listened. And the time for that is now over. *You,*" he poked Theo in the chest with his forefinger, "are a menace. A snake. You charm young women, vulnerable women, separating them from their families, stealing their money."

"I haven't stolen anyone's money, sir."

"Not yet you haven't, but you will, given time. That's what you're all about, you sorts. Breaking up families, gaining the trust of poor saps, leaving nothing but misery and broken relationships behind you." He looked over Theo's shoulder at his daughter as he spoke.

"I can assure you that's not what I want nor intend. Sally is free to leave us at any time. It is her right to do as she pleases."

"You've addled her mind!"

"She is an adult and she has chosen to remain here, sir."

"Only because you've brainwashed her. It's now time for her to come home. She needs to be where her mother and me can d—deprogram her or whatever it is we have to do to undo what you've done to her."

"Dad, it's not like that." Sally was pleading.

"We don't brainwash anyone, Richard. Everyone operates from free will here. We come and go as we please. We encourage each other to do so. We are the very opposite of brainwashed."

Theo was preternaturally calm, his expression cool, and his voice relaxed in the face of the seething older man. Venables' lips were pulled back as he bared his teeth like a hostile dog.

Scott stood to intervene. He was much larger and more threatening than Sally's father, but what the older man lacked in presence, he made up with fury and a father's protective instinct.

"Sit down!" he shouted at Scott. Scott glanced over to Theo. Theo shook his head, and Scott slowly sank back into his chair.

"Richard, we don't want any trouble, but you can't just come in here and kidnap your own daughter," Theo said.

"Why not? You did!"

"Come on, man, now you're being ridiculous. Calm down, and break some bread with us."

"I'm here to take my daughter home."

"Dad, please. You're embarrassing me."

"Come with me, Sally. Now!"

"It's your choice," Theo said to Sally. "You can stay or go. We will bless you whatever you choose."

The shocked audience watched the drama unfolding in silence, no one spoke. Sally looked wildly about her. She was blushing furiously, clenching and unclenching her fists. Her gaze flickered between the two men as she considered her choice.

"No, Dad. As I've said before, I'm staying here. You can't make me leave. I'm not a little girl anymore."

Her father growled and took a step. To stop him, Theo put his hand on the man's chest. Richard slapped it away. Scott stood then and walked over. He grabbed Venable's arm, his bulk and menace acting as a brake to prevent a fight from breaking out.

"You heard what she said. I think it better that you leave." Scott's voice rumbled low and quietly in his East Anglian burr.

Venables glared at Scott. He looked back at Sally, who had turned her back on her father. Julia comforted her.

Turning to Theo, Richard Venables cried out. "You, you are a coward and a psychopath! I will get you for this, taking my daughter away from me, upsetting her mother!" He spun on his heels to leave but quickly changed his mind and turned back. Taking Theo and Scott by surprise, Venables managed to land a left hook that knocked Theo to the ground.

Scott grabbed Venables by the arms and bundled him backwards, pinning him against the wall, the two men's faces just inches apart. Theo struggled to his feet, gingerly feeling his jaw. "Leave him. Just be on your way, Venables. You've no business here."

Venables shrugged himself out of Scott's grasp. "I'm going, I'm going. But I *will* get you."

He furiously pointed his finger at Theo before stumbling out of the room, closely followed by Scott. A moment later, they heard the front door clang shut. The atmosphere in the room relaxed, but only slightly.

Sally ran from the room, sobbing. Suki followed her. Theo let out a sigh. "Perhaps we should move again," he said, sitting down slowly.

"We can't do that!" It was Thomas. Theo looked at him in surprise. "I—I like it here," Thomas added quietly, looking down at the table.

Theo shrugged. "We may have to if he keeps on pestering us." Thomas, his eyes downcast, quietly picked up his spoon and resumed eating his dessert.

Julia reached into her pocket and pulled out Barnaby. She put him on the table. Even the little rabbit seemed wary, not straying far from his owner, despite the remnants of salad laying at the other end of the table.

CHAPTER NINE

ANNABELLE SAT ON Sally's bed in her messy room. Fallen plaster had left holes in the walls, and the air smelt damp. The tremendously high ceilings were draped with cobwebs. Despite this, Sally had made it as "girly" and presentable as she could.

Nets covered the heavy faded curtains, and old Christmas tree lights hung from the pelmet and around the room. Across her bed lay a quilt sewn from bright, randomly coloured, eight-inch squares. There was also a myriad of pillows and cushions at its head.

It was a dark room, but the evening summer sunlight streamed through the window. Dust motes bounced along on invisible air currents as birds chirruped outside as they prepared for dusk to fall. It was hot, and the atmosphere in the shabby room was stifling.

Sally leant forwards on a rickety wooden chair in front of a mirror, distorted, and spotted with age. She was putting on theatrical makeup. Black swooping eyebrows now extended far beyond her natural ones. A mask stretched across her eyes and nose. It was white, and she had painted tiny silver, purple, and black furls that curled and uncurled in intricate patterns across it. The design extended to her eyebrows and temples.

Sally had painted directly onto her skin with tiny brushes so that the line between mask and skin was barely discernible. Annabelle marvelled at her patience. The odd slick of lipstick was all she could manage, and even then it was rather a hit-and-miss affair.

"Does everyone go to this trouble?"

"Oh no, Julia will wear her mask plain. Suki might show up and ask me to paint her, it depends."

"What about the others? The men? What do they do?" After the scene in the dining room, Annabelle had felt obliged to stay. She had comforted Sally and watched her as her emotions stilled, her art calming her. Now her hands were steady, her eyes clear, and her brush strokes firm and confident.

"The men will wear different masks. The women represent St. Petrie, goodness, peace, and happiness. They are the light. The men dress up as Lord Darthamort. They represent justice, the punishment of all that is dark and evil."

"Two sides of the same coin."

"Exactly. Because Lord Darthamort is half-goat, half-man, the masks are more like headdresses. They are furry, bear-like. They cover their heads entirely, and they have real fur, feathers, horns, and teeth! The boys make them themselves from roadkill and the dead animals we find."

"That's quite something," Annabelle said. Sally looked in her mirror at Annabelle's reflection. "For vegans, I mean. Don't they object to putting something like that on their heads?"

"They don't. The masks are quite scary, and I think the

boys enjoy the opportunity to let loose. They really get into character. Well, Thomas doesn't, but Theo and Scott do. You'll see."

"I'm not sure I want to find out."

"Oh, it's fine. It's just a bit of fun! Just a group of grown-up kids, yelpin' and a-hollerin' around a bonfire."

There was a knock at the door, and Suki floated in. Her feet were bare. Pinned into her hair were small, white, star-shaped flowers.

"Your hair looks lovely," Sally said.

"Thank you. Jasmine smells so divine, I thought I'd carry it around with me. My hair seemed the perfect place for it." Suki brushed a tendril of her fine pale hair from her face. "Would you do my makeup, darling?"

Sally got up from her chair. She turned it to the window, gesturing for Suki to sit down. With the tip of her finger, she tilted Suki's chin upwards. Laid out on the table next to her was an array of makeup, brushes, and applicators. Sally dropped a fine brush into a tumbler of water, then dipped it into a tiny glass jar before leaning in and getting to work.

With her jaw set in concentration, Sally painted in silence except for gentle murmured instructions to Suki to look down or tilt her head to one side or the other. Suki, mindful that even the tiniest movement could spell disaster, did exactly as she was told and remained silent.

When Sally finally stepped back, Annabelle was amazed at the result. Suki wasn't wearing a mask at all. Sally had painted directly onto Suki's face.

Suki's eyes were enveloped in silver paint. It reached across Suki's upper and lower lids, winging out to her temples, into the corners of her eye sockets, and down her nose ending in sharp points. In the middle of Suki's forehead, Sally had painted a shining blue orb.

Directly above Suki's eyebrows and at the outer edges of her eyelids were blue and purple flowers. They added colour and a sense of glamour. Everything was joined by sweeping black lines that swooped and swirled in complex lattice patterns around Suki's eyes, showing off her clear, sky-blue irises. The black swirls continued across her nose, forehead, and down to the apples of her cheeks. Glitter and tiny sparkling jewel-coloured rhinestones finished off the effect. It was masterful, mysterious, and Annabelle had to admit, rather alluring.

"Golly, that's incredible!" she exclaimed.

"Would you like me to do you?" Sally asked.

"Oh, um, well, um . . ."

"It washes straight off."

Annabelle looked at the two brightly coloured, glamourous women and then at her plain, unadorned reflection in the black-spotted mirror.

"Oh, go on then. It can't hurt, just this once," Annabelle said, shutting out the negative voice in her head that sounded suspiciously like Philippa's.

Thirty minutes later, Annabelle had her own mask. Hers was lighter, brighter, and more colourful than Suki's. Like Suki, Sally had painted long, black swooping lines on Annabelle's face but blended yellow powder across her nose and cheeks.

From the ends of Annabelle's eyebrows to the middle of her cheekbones, red, purple, and blue powder curved in a "C" shape. Light blue, lilac, and pink were stroked across her brows. Gold dots added a three-dimensional effect.

A silver rhinestone in the middle of Annabelle's forehead was surrounded by six smaller ones. Then, Sally finished Annabelle's eyes with smoky grey and brown eye shadow, dramatic eyeliner, and lashings of mascara. She stood back.

Annabelle blinked rapidly, several times. She wasn't used to wearing eye makeup. She looked in the mirror at her reflection.

"Ohhhhhhhhhh," Annabelle could hardly believe who was looking back at her. "Ohhhhhh," she repeated, stunned. "It looks absolutely beautiful. Thank you." She turned her head to the right and left, examining Sally's work. "Gosh, is that really me?" She leant in closer to examine the fine detail of Sally's work. The black, gold, pinks, yellows, and blues made her eyes sparkle and pop, whilst her long, black eyelashes made them appear larger and appealing.

"Let's take a selfie!" Suki said.

Before Annabelle could grasp what was happening, Suki and Sally had crowded around her. Suki held out her phone and took one photo after another, adjusting the angles as she pouted and posed like an experienced model.

"Here, let's take Annabelle on her own. It's not every day a vicar gets to look like this. There has to be evidence!"

Suki and Sally moved away from Annabelle as quickly as they'd moved in, and Suki took more pictures, pressing the button on her phone repeatedly.

"Smile, Annabelle, smile!"

Annabelle smiled shyly. She felt a little awkward. "Throw your hair back, girlfriend! Flick it! Go on!"

"Well, I, er, don't norm—Oh, what the heck." Annabelle tossed her head and twisted her shoulders in poses she'd seen the other two women hold.

"That's it!" Suki called out, snapping away. "You can even pout, you know, push those lips out. Show us what you've got."

"Thank you," Annabelle said, standing up. "But I think that's enough, now."

"We've got to go, Sukes. It's nearly time," Sally said. "Is your mother joining us?" Sally tossed a white shift over her head and stepped into a pair of white slip-ons.

"Good grief, no. You know what she's like. Wouldn't be seen dead at such a thing. Give me your phone number, Annabelle. I'll text these to you."

The voice that sounded suspiciously like Philippa's was gaining momentum in Annabelle's head. She felt a little uncomfortable about what had just happened, but she gave Suki her number. Her phone pinged as the photos arrived.

"You go ahead, I'll catch up," Annabelle said. The two women hurried out of the door.

Annabelle sat down and opened up Suki's text. She had sent Annabelle five photos, two of the three of them, three of Annabelle on her own.

Annabelle scrolled back and forth between them, admiring Sally's work and marvelling at the glamour it bestowed upon all the women, but unsure it was entirely fitting for her, a woman of the cloth. There was one photo that caught her eye in particular. It was one of her by herself, a close-up, spontaneous. Her hair was back off her face, she must have "flicked it". She was looking at a point beyond the camera from one side, her mouth curved in just a hint of a smile. The light of the room combined with the colourful makeup to enhance the natural bright blue of her eyes and the pleasing contours of her face. Even Annabelle could see she looked quite lovely, radiant. A well of pride grew in her chest.

"Roger. I'll send it to Roger, he lives far enough away." Her brother lived on a remote Scottish island with his daughter. "Bonnie will find it fun, too."

CHAPTER TEN

THE BONFIRE RAGED in the middle of a clearing in the woods, far from the house. Yellow flames licked their way around the logs, branches, leaves, and twigs that members of the Brotherhood of St. Petrie had collected from the estate in the previous days. Sparks shot into the air. They glowed brightly against the black and blue sky as they rose, burning themselves out of existence on their downwards arc. Lanterns hung from trees, sparkling lights strung between them.

The group held hands in a line by the fire. The heat warmed their faces, the smell of smoke filled their nostrils, and, in Thomas' case, made him sneeze. The group swayed from side to side in unison, their eyes closed. They were humming quietly.

Annabelle felt her skin prickle. The bonfire continued to crackle and pop. Annabelle worried the fire might spread. Everything was so dry that it would take no more than a single spark to set off an inferno. The oppressive atmosphere of earlier had lifted, but the day's heat remained. In the distance, she heard a low rumble of thunder.

Annabelle sat on the stump of a tree some yards away. She had declined to partake in the ceremony, choosing to watch instead. Sally, Suki, and Julia were all dressed in white, their masks partially obscuring their faces. They looked fragile, ethereal, and other-worldly, especially next to their companions.

Thomas and Scott wore brown furry costumes. At their feet lay wooden clubs and long leather whips. A patchwork of matted grey and brown fur covered the fearsome head-gear they wore. One had small and beady eyes. Those on the other glowed green. Large, hooked plastic noses protruded below. Real, crusty horns curled outwards whilst wide, grinning mouths revealed many tiny, sharp teeth. Human eyes peered from behind them. Pheasant feathers fanned around their necks and flared out across their shoulders. The rich, speckled shades of brown and rust added some beauty, but not enough. They looked fiend-like, grotesque, devastating.

The group in front of the fire was getting louder now, swaying more wildly, their eyes closed. They dropped hands and moved apart. Scott picked up a drum made from animal skin stretched across a wooden barrel. He began to thump it slowly, creating a low, steady beat. Suki banged a huge metal triangle with a stick. Julia strummed a tiny banjo. It was a cacophony of tuneless, random sounds.

Barnaby poked out from Julia's pocket, his little head popping up shyly before bobbing out of sight again. Sally and Thomas continued to sway to the music, Thomas moving self-consciously. Even though the men were clad head to foot in costume, their movements gave them away. Scott, for all his bulk, had rhythm, whilst Thomas had none.

Deep in the trees, a voice boomed. It was Theo. He was suspended high in a tree, standing on a platform. He still had on the shirt and jeans he had been wearing earlier. By his feet was a Darthamort mask.

At the sound of his voice, the others stopped their noise. They stood still, waiting as Theo, his feet apart, held a large, smoked glass bowl high in front of him. He was chanting something Annabelle couldn't quite hear. There was a suede baton in his hand. A deep, booming note resounded from the bowl as he hit it gently. It vibrated in the air, the sound getting louder as the seconds passed before eventually fading.

Theo set aside the bowl. He cupped his hands around his mouth to shout over the noise of the crackling fire. "Dear followers, we gather here to celebrate St. Petrie and his brother, Lord Darthamort. We honour their blessings and worship their souls. We praise them, we praise all living things that show us what it is to be sentient beings, of what is good and right." Theo dropped his hands and looked down. He caught sight of Annabelle and smiled. "We are further blessed this evening by the presence of the mighty Reverend Annabelle Dixon." Annabelle shifted awkwardly on the tree trunk, uncomfortable at being incorporated into this strange ritual and unsure where it was leading. "Her presence shows us that we are on the right path."

Annabelle sat bolt upright. She started to object, raising her arm, pointing a finger skywards. "Hey, I say, that's . . ."

But Theo carried on. He raised his face to the now dark, starless sky, his arms outstretched, his eyes closed. "Join us, join us, Lord Darthamort, St. Petrie. Guide us, your faithful servants to your glory. Praise be, praise the Lord, Lord Darthamort. Amen."

Annabelle jumped up indignantly and stood on the tree

stump. "Stop! Stop!" She shouted, but a bone-shaking roll of thunder drowned out her voice.

The sky lit up as a streak of lightning tore across it. The group around the bonfire yelled in unison. "Praise be! Praise the Lord! Lord Darthamort! Amen!"

They each reached down and threw something into the fire. In the darkness, Annabelle was almost blind but snatched a glimpse of a shadowy shape projected against the backlight of the flames. Horseshoes. They were throwing horseshoes. As they released them into the fire, the group ran, scattering into the trees, whooping, screaming, and yelling. Annabelle watched them wide-eyed, her fists clenched. She was left alone by the bonfire. Another flash of lightning split the sky.

There was a roar at Annabelle's shoulder. She screamed. She leapt off the tree stump and stepped back. Bright green eyes shone brightly at her. White teeth stood out in the gloom. There was a cackle, a voice Annabelle recognised as Scott's. Having scared her, he disappeared into the trees. Annabelle, unwilling to be caught off-guard again, looked in all directions. A shriek pierced the air followed by a laugh. Annabelle wondered if she was being silly. Perhaps she needed to lighten up. She started to walk into the woods.

Every few yards, young, spindly saplings were interspersed with older trees, their large brown trunks providing good coverage and hiding places. Annabelle weaved in and out, catching sight of flashes of white whilst hearing footsteps and rustling, roars and squeals, as the shadowy hunters and their pale prey ran between trees and behind bushes. The sounds of leather slapped against tree trunks travelled through the air. Annabelle lurched towards the sounds, rebounding through the trees like pinballs permanently in play. Disoriented, she stumbled as flashes of lightning and rumbles of thunder continued to clash violently overhead.

A Darthamort ran up to her, roaring just feet from her face. He whipped his leather rope on the ground, slicing fallen leaves in two. This time, Annabelle had no intention of balking at this attempt at intimidation. She smartly stepped aside behind a tree trunk, hiding her fear with an upturned chin and quick footwork. Again, a whip cracked against the ground, followed by footsteps as he ran off.

Annabelle had had just about enough of this. Philippa was right. This "celebration" was a silly, mischievous joke at best, an evil, manipulative stunt dressed up as an honourable, righteous ritual at worst. She thought back to the scene with the furious Richard Venables. Perhaps Theo was the kind of person to prey on souls looking for redemption. Perhaps he targeted them and led them astray.

Annabelle stalked through the woods towards Lolly Lane. The ground underfoot was bumpy and covered with low brush. More than once her feet were ambushed and snared by wiry vines like animals in a trap. Annabelle blindly pressed on, driven by her desire to get home to safety, warmth, and comfort. Branches brushed her face, startling her.

Finally, when she could no longer hear the roars and screams through the trees, she saw the lights of the Hamilton's and Cuddy's homes. Thank goodness, not too much longer now. Ooof! Annabelle flew through the air. She landed on her front with a thud, closing her mouth too late. Gasping, spitting leaves and dirt, she pushed herself to her hands and knees.

She could see a shadowy outline behind her and gingerly put out her hand to pat the lump. It was soft but inert. Under her hand, she felt fur, rough, wiry, sharp even. She felt tiny, hard, jagged teeth. Her eyes widened in the dark as she attempted to see. She frantically moved her hands around, patting the features she could feel under her fingertips. When she felt the bony curves of two horns, she jumped to her feet with a yelp. Above her, another flash of lightning lit up the woods. Then it all went black again.

Annabelle sat on the ground. She could no longer see what faced her, but she knew what was there. For in the flash of light the storm had provided, Annabelle had seen what had brought her down. She now sat next to a gruesome sight, a body lying on the forest floor, his arms outstretched. He lay as though in sacrifice to the saviours he worshiped.

Annabelle leant over to wrestle off his headgear as another streak of lightning lit her up. Large, fat raindrops plopped down onto the face. The man didn't flinch. His face had settled into a different kind of mask. As the light disappeared again, Annabelle peered around, looking for help, a clue, anything. She listened, hoping to hear noises above the sounds of the thunder, but she heard nothing. Even the squeals and the cracks of whips had ceased.

Annabelle sat on her haunches, covering the wound with her hands, willing for there to be movement beneath them. But it was hopeless. In the woods, among the trees and the animals, under the black, oppressive sky, Theo Westmoreland was quite dead, a small, black mark in the centre of his chest.

CHAPTER ELEVEN

THERE COULD BE no doubt, the placement of his wound was too precise. Theo had been brutally murdered. Annabelle dropped her head to pray, but behind her, bushes rustled. Her heart jumped. She turned to the sound to see Thomas, a camera on a strap around his neck. He was no longer in costume, and as he raised his camera to his face, light from his flash lit up the scene before him.

"Reverend—" he stopped abruptly. "What's going on?" His voice rose to a falsetto on the last syllable.

"Theo has come a cropper," Annabelle said, her voice shaking.

Thomas crouched. "Is he d–dead?" His hand hovered over Theo's body.

"Looks to me like he was shot, once through the chest. Probably killed him instantly." Annabelle looked at Thomas carefully. Thomas's hand continued to hover above Theo's body. His breathing was heavy.

"Who c–could have done this?" he said.

"We must call the police. And gather up the others."

"Listen, it's q–quiet now. The rain m–must have sent them indoors. They'll be sheltering inside."

Annabelle punched 999 into her phone. "Police, please." She was put through. "I'd like to report a suspicious death." She gave the details to the operator and hung up.

"What should we do n–now?" Thomas asked her.

"Well, I need to stay with the body until the police arrive. You could go up to the house."

"If I do that, I'll h–have to tell them what happened. I don't think I could do that, Vicar."

"Fair enough. Let's put that off until we have to."

They moved over to a fallen tree and sat next to one another to wait. The tops of the trees above them were providing good cover against the rain, but steadily their clothes and hair became plastered to their bodies.

"You're wearing regular clothes," Annabelle said. "What happened to your costume?"

"What? Oh, I took my c–costume off as soon as we ran into the trees. I always do that. I've no interest in running around chasing people, scaring them. Not my th–thing at all."

"So what have you been doing?"

"What I always do, Reverend." Thomas grasped his camera. "P–pictures. I got some great night shots, especially of the s–storm."

They heard a shout followed by sounds of people walking through brush. Leaves parted, and Sally and Scott appeared a few yards away, beams of light from torches illuminating their path. Sally had removed her mask. Scott had dispensed with his headdress but not his costume. Annabelle jumped up, putting her hands to her face to protect her eyes as the light from Scott's torch immediately found her.

"Have you seen Theo?" Sally asked. "He hasn't turned up at the house." It must have been raining hard beyond the trees because both Scott and Sally were drenched. Strings of hair framed Sally's face and her white skirt clung.

"Yes, um . . ." Sally took a step towards Annabelle. "Don't come any further, Sally!"

"What is it? What have you got there?" Sally peered around Annabelle at the figure on the floor.

"Is that—? Is that— Theo! Oh, my gosh! Theo!"

Sally lurched forwards, but Scott grabbed her. She struggled against him, but he held her firmly around her waist.

"I'm very sorry." Annabelle's voice was gentle.

"Is he dead, Vicar?" Scott's voice was gruff.

"I'm afraid he is."

The sound of Sally's wail rose as she sagged against Scott, who struggled to hold her upright.

"We're waiting for the police. They'll be here soon."

"Who found him?" Scott asked, his voice still low and hoarse.

"I did. I tripped over him on my way back to my car." Sally let out another wail.

"Calm down, Sally lass," Scott urged her. Sally pulled herself furiously out of Scott's grasp and sat cross-legged on the ground among the leaves. She put her head in her hands like a petulant child before exclaiming, "Oh, but what about Suki? And Margaret? They need to know. We must tell them! Oh, poor, poor Theo!" Sally looked at Scott frantically.

"They mustn't come down here. It's a potential crime scene," Annabelle said.

"A crime scene?"

"He may have been killed deliberately. Shot," Thomas said, provoking another wail from Sally.

Scott put his hands on his head. "No, no, no."

"You must keep the others away, Scott," Annabelle reiterated.

He nodded. "I'll make sure they stay up at the house."

"I'll come with you," Thomas said. He helped Sally up, took her other side, and the three of them stumbled their way back through the trees, leaving Annabelle alone in the woods with the body once more.

She shivered and looked around. She scrubbed at her face with a mixture of leaves and grass, hoping to remove the makeup, which now seemed wholly inappropriate. Her phone pinged. She looked down. It was a text from Mike. He'd sent her a photo of the dogs lying by the fire in her cottage. He'd taken it the day before he left for his conference. Annabelle smiled.

`What are you doing?`

Annabelle looked over at Theo's body.

`Sitting in the woods with a dead body for company.`

Annabelle pressed the back button repeatedly before retyping her message.

`Just sitting around. You?`

A few seconds later, her phone pinged again.

`Finished my homework. Ready for tomorrow's`

session on The Role of Counter-Drones in
Rural and Community Policing. Bound to be
riveting. Now to bed. Early start.

Goodnight, Mike. Sleep tight.

You too, Annabelle. Don't do anything I
wouldn't do.

Annabelle pursed her lips in a rueful smile.

I'll try not to.

She put the phone down and waited. She could hear
the wail of sirens in the far distance.

CHAPTER TWELVE

THE POLICE DETECTIVE striding towards Annabelle wasn't Mike, that was for sure. He was older, sturdier, and he wore a trilby hat. He did wear the same trench coat, however. Annabelle wondered if the dark grey raincoat came as part of the uniform. She watched the policeman nervously. She felt a little shaken and mistrustful, unable to discern who was friend and who was foe. However, she was glad the loneliness of waiting had been replaced by the bustle of a murder investigation in full swing.

The detective stood in front of her, his feet apart, his arms folded. "So, you're the local vicar? The one who found the body?" His voice was gravelly, his eyes unfriendly. He looked her up and down, and Annabelle wondered if her attempts at removing her makeup had been successful.

"Yes, that's right, Inspector . . . ?"

"Chief Inspector. Ainslie, Brian Ainslie."

"We normally get Inspector Nicholls."

"Get a lot of murders around here, do you?" Ainslie

squinted at Annabelle. "Nicholls is away, so you've got me for your troubles. Now tell me, Vicar, what do you know?"

The chief inspector got out a notebook and pencil, an increasingly rare sight. Even Mike had upgraded to a tablet after Annabelle pointed out he'd spend less time behind a desk if he did. "You don't use a tablet, Chief Inspector?"

"Nope. When I was in the field back in the day, paper and pen did me alright. And they'll do me fine again." Annabelle waited as he licked the end of his pencil and readied himself to write down her words. "Now, how did you come to find the body?"

"I tripped over it as I was making my way back to my car. It was, is, parked in Lolly Lane. I couldn't see well in the dark, and oof, there he was."

"Hmph. You seem very calm about it."

"When you're in my line of work, Chief Inspector, you see all sorts. This isn't, unfortunately, my first murder investigation."

Ainslie stared at her, narrowing his eyes. "Seems a strange place for a vicar to be at this time of an evening. What were you doing here? Were you part of . . . with these . . . *people*?" He waved in the direction of the big house behind him. In the distance, she could see the remains of the bonfire that earlier had been fierce, flaming. Only glowing embers remained.

"The group, the brotherhood, invited me to their celebration."

"The who? The what?"

"The Brotherhood of St. Petrie. That's what they call themselves. The people who live in the big house."

"The Brotherhood of . . . ? What on earth's that when it's at home?"

"That's what I was here to find out, Chief Inspector. It

seems they live here in a sort of commune under the auspices of doing good in their local community. I came to find out more about them. They've been wandering through the village and putting the wind up the locals a little."

"Is that so? In what way exactly?"

"Oh, they just chat, give out flowers, sell a few things. Nothing harmful. They're strangers though, and the villagers are always suspicious of strangers, especially when they act and dress so differently. You know how it is in small communities."

"More of a city man, meself."

Annabelle relayed to the chief inspector everything she'd learnt about the group, including a description of the ceremony they had performed earlier.

"A bunch of weirdos, then."

"Well, I wouldn't—"

"And this chap, what do you know about him?" The detective thumbed in the direction of Theo's body. It had been covered with a white tent. "Nothing really. He seemed charming, a little fervent perhaps, a little manipulative, but relatively harmless."

"Any enemies?"

"Really, I have no idea, Chief Inspector. I only met him a few hours ago."

The detective wrote her words down, ending his writing with a decisive flourish, and looked up. "Hmph, right, Vicar. That will be all for now. You may go up to the house and wait there until my sergeant has taken your statement. It seems clear to me that the murderer must be one of the people out here at the time, and seeing as you were one of them, you can't be discounted."

"Excuse me, Chief Inspector! Are you saying that I am a suspect?"

"Can't rule you out, Vicar. You have no alibi, so you will just have to wait it out in the house until we're through. I'm sure it's nothing, but for now, please humour me."

The flaps on the white tent parted, and out stepped the local pathologist, Harper Jones. She spoke to a constable standing guard who pointed to Annabelle and the detective. She acknowledged them with a tip of her chin and walked over.

"Good evening, Chief Inspector, Reverend," she said, looking at them both before addressing Ainslie. "Harper Jones, I'm the local bones." They shook hands. "Reverend?"

"I found the body," Annabelle said simply.

"What can you tell us, Dr. Jones?" Ainslie asked.

Harper swung her gaze from Annabelle to Ainslie and gave a summary without pausing for breath.

"He was shot through the chest from close range. Death would have been instantaneous. The wound is unusual, though. Not the typical shotgun injury that you'd expect in these parts."

"Time of death? He was seen around ten p.m. and then this vicar lady here found him shortly afterwards."

"That sounds about right. I'll have more for you in the morning. We'll remove the body now. We're done here."

Harper gave Annabelle a warning look. "Take care of yourself, Reverend." She walked away, peeling off her paper crime scene suit as she walked to her car. Annabelle hesitated but seeing the chief inspector looking at her squarely made her realise she had no option but to follow Harper away from the crime scene and on up to the house.

CHAPTER THIRTEEN

M ARGARET WESTMORELAND WAS again sitting in the deckchair on the steps outside the kitchen. She was much as Annabelle had found her earlier, except that now her hair was rumpled, and she looked as though she had aged ten years. It was dark, the only lights being the red glow from the end of a cigarette as Margaret pulled on it, her hands shaking, and that of the moon. The rain had stopped. Theo's mother clutched a coat around her. On the ground sat Suki wearing an oversized cardigan. She used the long sleeves to wipe her face as tears streamed down it silently. Her head was in her mother's lap. Margaret stroked her daughter's hair and stared blankly ahead.

"I'm so terribly sorry for your loss, Margaret," Annabelle said. The older woman didn't look at her but waved her cigarette around, causing flakes of smouldering ash to fly into the air.

Suki lifted her head. "Who could have done this, Annabelle?" she cried. "Th–Theo was a friend to everyone." *Sally's father wasn't too keen on him.*

Margaret dragged on her cigarette. She had an empty tumbler in her hand. On the floor next to her was a bottle of gin. It was almost empty. Margaret picked it up by the neck and unsteadily sloshed what was left into her glass.

"Get me some ice, would you?" She waved the tumbler at Annabelle. Annabelle ignored Margaret's impertinence and took the glass from her, went into the kitchen, and over to the fridge. She opened the icebox and picked out the ice cube tray, holding it over the glass as she popped a couple of cubes into it.

"What did you tell the police?" Margaret asked when Annabelle came outside again. The heat had dropped now that the storm had moved on, but it was still warm enough to comfortably sit outside despite it being nearly midnight.

"I told them what I saw, that I was observing the ritual, and that everyone disappeared into the woods. I didn't hear anything except people yelling and screaming. And I didn't see anything that would pertain to . . . to Theo's death."

"That stupid legend." Margaret jabbed her cigarette into the ashtray perched on the stone balustrade beside her. She lit another. "Someone was always going to get hurt. All that heightened emotion, running around, screaming. And those ridiculous masks offering anonymity. It was asking for trouble."

"But Mama, the others said that Theo was shot!" Suki looked wildly at Annabelle. "Shot! We don't have any guns. How could it have happened?" Suki stopped. "Perhaps it was a poacher? Someone shooting rabbits. That could be it. It could, couldn't it, Annabelle?"

Annabelle seriously doubted it, but the alternative was to point out that Theo had been murdered and probably by one of the people he lived among. "The police will find out who did it, Suki. I'm quite sure of that."

"Hmph," Margaret squinted as she pulled again on her cigarette but made no other comment.

Annabelle decided to leave them with their grief and ventured into the house to find the others. She could hear the sounds of Sally still wailing. She found a bathroom and splashed water on her face, washing off the remnants of makeup that remained. Her earlier antics seemed foolish now.

The police had commandeered the former drawing room as their interview suite. Two police constables that Annabelle didn't recognise stood at the doorway. Inside, she found Sally comforted by Scott, who still had his arm around her shoulders. Sally was leaning with her elbows on her knees, her hands covering her face as she sobbed into them. Thomas came up to Annabelle as she walked into the room.

"She's devastated."

"Yes, I can see. Perhaps I can help."

Thomas stepped aside, and Annabelle crouched down next to Sally. "I'm so sorry, Sally. I know you held Theo in very high regard."

"I *loved* him!" Sally raised her head from her hands. "Oh, he didn't love me, but that doesn't matter now. I *adored* him." Scott started, but he didn't take his eyes off Sally. He merely clasped one of her hands.

"Who could have done this? Who?" Sally repeated. "Theo was one of the nicest, most charming, most compassionate men you could ever meet. He couldn't have been kinder to me when I first arrived. He was always willing to help out in the kitchen, and he was so clever. He did all the accounts!"

Annabelle kept her expression neutral. "It *is* truly

devastating, Sally. I'm sure the police will do all they can to find out who did this."

Sally looked into Annabelle's eyes. "Do you think, oh my gosh, do you think it was my *dad*?" Both Thomas and Scott looked away, but Annabelle held Sally's gaze. "I don't know. I'm sure the police will question him and get to the truth." She turned to Scott. "Do you know where Richard went, Scott? After you led him out?"

Keeping one arm around Sally, Scott spread his other hand wide. "No idea. I watched him stumble down the driveway and into the woods." Sally gave a little squeal and hid her face in her hands again. "After he disappeared, I came back inside."

"D–Do you know . . . Was he really shot?" Sally said.

"It looks like he was, yes."

Relief flooded Sally's face, and her shoulders relaxed. "Well, there you are then. It couldn't have been Dad. He doesn't know how to use a gun. I doubt he's ever even held one." She stopped squeezing her tissue for a moment. "But if it wasn't Dad, then who was it?" She started working on the tissue again. "I mean, if it wasn't him, it could have been one of us?" Sally looked at the two men in turn. Scott leant forwards, his feet apart, his elbows on his thighs. Thomas stood a few feet away, leaning against the large stone fireplace, his hands in his pockets.

Sally jumped up, a look of fear and disgust on her face. "I'm not sitting here. I'm leaving. Who knows what kind of monster I'm sharing this house with?"

"You'll do no such thing, ma'am," a commanding female voice boomed. A tall, slim woman with cropped blonde hair walked into the room. She wore a grey, short-sleeved T-shirt over a white long-sleeved one and black cargo pants. She looked fit, sharp, and trim. Annabelle's first thought was to wonder how she could wear cargo pants and still look stylish. She had tried on a pair once. Her reflection in the changing room mirror had come back to her in her nightmares. Accompanying the policewoman were Julia, Suki, and Margaret.

"You're all to stay here. This is a crime scene. Until we find out who committed this heinous act, Chief Inspector Ainslie has instructed that you are to stay on the estate," the woman said. She spoke in a South London accent.

"What? Even me?" The words were out before Annabelle registered she was saying them.

The woman eyed Annabelle. "Yes, even you."

"But this is The Reverend Annabelle Dixon from St. Mary's in the village," Suki said. "Surely, you can't think . . ."

The officer looked Annabelle up and down. Annabelle felt the colour rise in her cheeks. The woman's face remained implacable, however, and it was clear Suki's entreaty would have no effect.

"Look, my name is Scarlett Lawrence. I'm the sergeant running this case with Chief Inspector Ainslie, and if he says you're all to stay here, then you're all to stay here, got it?" Everyone except Margaret nodded.

"Now, I'm going to call you over and take your statements, one by one. When I've done you, you're free to leave the room, but you have to stay in the house, alright?"

"But what should we do, Sergeant?" Suki lamented. She sighed, standing on one foot, wrapping the other around her ankle. She tilted her head.

The woman rolled her eyes. "It's late. Go to bed. That's what I would do. Now, hand me your phones. You'll get them back when the chief says so."

Amidst much muttering and sighing, the seven of them

handed their phones over. Sergeant Lawrence dragged an old chair over to a table in the corner of the room. As they waited, they sat in silence some yards away on faded, dusty couches, except for Thomas, who stood looking out of the window over the lawn and the woods beyond.

Margaret sat stoic and upright on a *chaise longue*, the fabric depicting, if one looked closely, scenes of the hunt; a fox chased by hounds and red-coated men on horseback. Next to her, Suki still dressed in diaphanous white, held her hand. Across from them, sitting on an equally faded, pale green couch was Sally. She looked exhausted and despondent. Next to her was Scott. He looked down at his lap, his lips pursed, his arms folded. Julia perched stiffly on the edge of the couch next to him. Annabelle stood next to the fireplace looking at the forlorn group around her, her arms behind her back. It was not a happy scene.

As she promised, Sergeant Lawrence called them over one by one, and took their statements. After they had read and signed them, each person filed out of the room without speaking or looking back.

Only Annabelle stayed. Despite her efforts, she fell into a doze on the couch. She awoke sometime later when there was a bang and a subsequent clang as a door was pushed open and left to close under its weight. Chief Inspector Ainslie stormed in, his bulk creating an updraft.

"Okay, give the vicar her phone back, and she can go," he said to his sergeant. He thumbed at Annabelle. "I spoke to Nicholls. He vouched for you."

With her back to them, Annabelle's eyes widened at the sound of Mike's name. Her heart swelled a little. Ainslie walked around to her. "You can go home, Vicar. But make sure you check in with us tomorrow, okay? We're close to arresting someone, but you're not out of the woods yet." He chuckled at his little joke.

"Arresting someone? Already?"

"Yeah, open-and-shut case, no doubt about it. You were here. There was an altercation tonight, wasn't there? Between the father of one of the women and the victim. A Richard Venables. We had more than one statement that described how he threatened the deceased. We've not picked him up yet, but we will. We have officers combing the woods and the local area for him, so it won't be long."

"I see, Chief Inspector. Well, if I can be of any help, please let me know."

"A quick word with the big man up top wouldn't go amiss, Vicar, but we practically have it in the bag." Ainslie was positively loquacious now that he had a strong lead, and he clapped Annabelle on the shoulder as he pushed her out the door into the night.

"Can one of my lads help you to your car?"

"That would be very kind, Chief Inspector."

"Raven!" he yelled at Constable Jim Raven, one of the local bobbies standing by a patrol car on the gravel drive-way. "Take the kind vicar back to her vehicle, would you?"

"Of course, Chief Inspector."

"Thanks, Jim. It's next to the Cuddy's in Lolly Lane. It seems an awfully long time ago that I left it there."

"It's been quite a night, hasn't it, Reverend?"

"It certainly has, Jim. It certainly has."

CHAPTER FOURTEEN

ANNABELLE OPENED HER eyes and stared at the ceiling. The previous night's events slowly seeped into her mind like the spread of a puddle below a dripping pipe. When she had arrived home, she turned on her phone and confronted a stream of texts from Mike. They variously communicated his horror at her situation, concern for her well-being, and frustration at her ability to get into all kinds of trouble. She had replied calmly to reassure him and to thank him for his help. Because he had vouched for her, she had been able to sleep in her own bed, something for which she was incredibly grateful.

Biscuit pushed open the bedroom door and padded into the room. The cat jumped onto the bed and broke Annabelle's early morning reverie by nonchalantly walking across her stomach. "Oof. Don't mind me, Biscuit."

The ginger tabby squeezed her eyes shut as Annabelle rubbed her finger down the cat's nose. Biscuit then folded her front paws and pinned Annabelle to the bed by settling on her chest.

"Maybe I'm finally getting somewhere with you, pussy-cat," Annabelle said.

With Biscuit's face not far from her own, Annabelle thought about Theo, his charm, his attractiveness, his magnetism, and his followers. Whilst they were certainly strange and a little disconcerting, the members of the brotherhood didn't appear harmful. A bunch of people acting a little oddly, that was all. But none of them had alibis. Any one of them in the woods could have murdered Theo.

Margaret, meanwhile, had been alone at the house. She had been cool about her son's death, but Annabelle knew from extensive experience that people grieved differently. She wasn't inclined to put too much store by Margaret's reaction. However, her indifference when Annabelle arrived at the house earlier marked Margaret out as a complicated woman. Still, it was hard to believe that she might kill her son.

And who could blame Richard Venables for holding a grudge against Theo? His daughter was a grown woman and entitled to make her own decisions, but Annabelle could conceive how Sally moving away, living an unconventional life, distancing herself from her family, and possibly giving away her money might make a father feel. Annabelle had to admit that Venables' outburst and the threat he had levelled at Theo the previous evening made him the prime suspect. Nevertheless, something about the chief inspector's insistence that he must be the murderer unsettled her. Annabelle sighed and gave Biscuit one last apologetic scrub between the ears.

"Sorry, kitty, time for me to get up."

Annabelle had a rehearsal for the show later that day. Directing the children in a coherent musical arrangement would require all her energy. She would need to put Theo's murder out of her mind. Her phone pinged. It was a text from Mike.

```
Let the police do their jobs, Annabelle.
Stay out of it.
```

She smiled. Mike knew her well. Now, though, he was reading her mind.

Annabelle hurried down her garden path and opened the gate. She didn't want to be late for rehearsal. The last time that had happened, she had arrived at the village hall to find Johnny Curnoweth shinning up the drainpipe to join three of his friends on the roof. Inside the hall, the situation had been no better. It had taken her half an hour to bring the rowdy youngsters under control.

As she banged the gate shut and turned to hurry the short distance to the hall, she pulled herself up abruptly to avoid bumping into the man coming along the pavement.

"Chief Inspector Ainslie! What are you doing here?"

"I was just coming to tell you, Vicar. We apprehended Richard Venables last night. We've got our man."

"Is that so? Please walk with me. I'm on my way to rehearsal, and the children will literally be climbing the walls if I'm late. Tell me what happened."

The chief inspector fell into step beside her. "We found him hiding in the woods. Not far from the house. He'd parked his car on a path that runs through the trees. He was fast asleep! Put up no resistance at all when we arrested him. As I said last night, open-and-shut case. Threatening the victim, proximity to where the victim was found. We have him banged to rights."

"Well, you certainly seem to have motive and opportunity, Chief Inspector. But what about the murder weapon? Any sign of that?"

"Bones, Dr. Jones, said he was killed with some kind of bolt through the heart. We haven't found the weapon yet, but we're on it. Anyhow, Reverend, the killer has been taken into custody, and your villagers can sleep safely in their beds. Tell them, Vicar, tell them the good news!" The chief inspector raised his hand and waved as he peeled away to his car, leaving her to shake her head as she continued to walk down the street.

The rehearsal was bedlam. Even the oldest children, Trevor Bligh and Caroline Lowen were disruptive. When Annabelle found them, they were arguing over whether the part of Joseph could be played by a female.

"Cross-gender acting is perfectly acceptable, Trevor! The Greeks did it, Shakespeare did it. Pantomime dames are played by men all the time!"

Trevor rolled his eyes. "Yeah, and they're ridiculous! We're meant to laugh at them. This is the *Bible*. You can't have a man played by a *girl*."

At the other end of the hall, Billy Breville charged around, his arms, having escaped from their slings, outspread. He was making loud aeroplane noises and inciting several other boys to do the same. One of them was Nicholas Pettit whose four-year-old sister, Maisie was playing the part of "Sheep." A lively girl, Maisie was not to be outdone by her brother. Her attempts at keeping up with him were proving fraught, however, as the three boys in battle formation turned to go back the way they had come, oblivious to the little girl coming up behind them. Confronted with three ten-year-old boys running towards her at speed, Maisie put her fists up to fight. A sheep, little Maisie was not.

Annabelle clapped her hands. "Children! Children!" The kids ignored her, continuing to career around the room and make a lot of noise. Annabelle started a rhythmic clap that Mrs. Bellon, the primary school teacher, had taught her. It had been a lifesaver. In a few seconds, all the children were standing still, or at least, as in Maisie's case, had slowed down. They mirrored the clap, slapping their hands together in unison until they had all calmed down.

"Now then, children! Gather together. You know what to do."

The children moved to the centre of the room and shuffled around until they lined up in rows. The sopranos were on the right, the altos on the left. Smaller ones at the front, taller ones at the back. The very little ones, of which there were eight, roamed around in no particular order at the front. Annabelle's only expectations of them were that they look adorable and not disrupt the proceedings too much.

Annabelle tapped her music stand with her baton. When she had come up with the idea for the show, she had hoped Mr. Fenwick, her choirmaster, would take on the task of directing but he had gone so pale when she mentioned it that Annabelle thought he might have a stroke. She was beginning to understand why.

Annabelle surveyed the children. "Goodness me! We have been in the wars."

Sitting on a chair was eleven-year-old Tabitha Brunswick. She had a bandage wrapped around her head. There were crutches propped against the wall next to her. Her mother was hovering, anxious to leave but worried that another calamity might befall her child if she did so.

In the middle row, Billy Breville's black eye was now golden and black. He still had casts on both wrists. They were now adorned with what looked like graffiti but which were, in fact, the early efforts of multiple ten-year-olds producing a signature.

Chloe Simmons had a nasty bruise on her elbow and two bandaged fingers. George Cracker had his arm in a sling. Nancy Rinker was wearing orthopaedic boots on *both* feet. And Timmy Trebuthwick had nasty grazes on his right shin and forearm as though he had been dragged.

"Let's go over the colours again."

Annabelle walked to a large metal cupboard that had once housed stock items for the local shop but was now home to Sunday school paraphernalia. On the front of it, on a large piece of butcher's paper, Annabelle had written in big, red letters the words to one of the songs they had been struggling with. It was a long list of colours. She'd hoped to get away without using such prompts in the final performance. But when she had tried to get the children to sing the list by heart, the results had been farcical, and no amount of practice had improved the situation. Many of the children could only remember up to the fourth colour and simply mumbled to the halfway point before giving up entirely after that. It was left to one child, Hermione Plaistell, a pious, overconfident thirteen-year-old to sing to the end. Unfortunately, more often than not, Hermione finished on an off-key high note that was simply impossible to ignore.

"Remember, breathe at the end of the rows, kiddos.

Here, here, and here." Annabelle tapped her baton on the paper.

"Deep breath, now." Annabelle breathed in through her nose. The children did likewise. The vicar had taught them to breathe deeply and let the air out slowly as they recited the list. Even that had not gone smoothly. At the previous rehearsal, Jud Whitworth had held his breath for so long that he had gone bright red, and then blue before fainting onto the wooden parquet flooring.

"And! Red and yellow and pink . . ."

The assembled children, grim determination on their faces, began to sing the many colours of Joseph's multi-coloured dream coat. As they had been taught, they took deep, noisy breaths at the end of every other row, their energy wound tightly as they focused on getting through the song, preferably without collapsing.

CHAPTER FIFTEEN

EVENTUALLY, THE REHEARSAL was over. The children went home, leaving Annabelle to potter about the hall, stacking chairs and picking up litter in restorative silence. As she peeled off a green boiled sweet stuck to the wall, Annabelle heard footsteps behind her. She turned to see Constable Raven. He was chewing his lip.

"Constable? Jim? Are you alright?"

Raven had taken off his police cap. He turned it in his hands whilst he frowned and pursed his lips.

"Yes, I'm alright, Vicar. We got that guy, you know. Venables."

"Yes, the Chief Inspector told me earlier. He seemed quite certain that Mr. Venables is the murderer."

"He is that, for sure." Raven twisted the cap in his hand with some violence now, turning each hand in opposite directions. "Certain, I mean."

"But . . . ? You're not?" Annabelle nodded at the cap in Jim's hands. "You're going to ruin the structure of that hat if you're not careful. It will never be the same." Jim immediately stopped his fidgeting.

"Oh, I don't know, Vicar. Everyone's cock-a-hoop down at the station. And he does have a motive."

"And opportunity."

"Yeah, that too. But, oh, I don't know . . ." Annabelle waited as Raven paused. He looked at the ceiling and then down at his feet. "There's something funny. At the house. Nobody's paying it any attention, but I think it's important. They're overlooking something."

"Oh?"

"Look, if I show you, will you promise not to tell anyone?"

"You know I can't do that, not if it's something relevant to the investigation. And if it is relevant, shouldn't you be telling the Chief Inspector? Or at least, his sergeant?"

"I have told them. They know about it. But they're not interested in following up. It may not be anything, but I'm concerned we have the wrong man. We don't have the murder weapon yet, and so far no concrete evidence to connect Venables to the killing."

Annabelle took a half-eaten sandwich left on the piano's keys between two fingers. She dropped it in the bin.

"It may well have been him, but there's another line of inquiry I think we should pursue," Raven persisted.

Annabelle straightened up. Raven looked tired and strained. Gone was the jovial community copper who loved kicking a ball around with local lads, who delighted six-year-olds at the village school by bringing Cleopatra, the police dog, into class.

Annabelle picked up the final chair. Someone had tipped it over.

"Here, let me do that for you, Vicar." Raven took the chair from her and stacked it on the pile next to the piano.

"Alright, Jim, let's do it," Annabelle said, coming to a decision. "Let's go to the house, and you can show me whatever it is. But I'm not promising to keep it a secret. Not if I think it important."

"Thanks, Vicar, I appreciate it. I've brought the car with me. We can go up there now if you like.

Raven drove the sole police car assigned to the village force slowly through the streets and out into the countryside beyond. The sun shone brightly, and the sky was a clear, crystal blue. The rolling fields on either side were a mixture of crops and pasture, broken up by the hedgerows and trees that stretched outwards to the horizon. Annabelle thought that from where God sat, the countryside must look like a massive, irregularly patched green blanket, all sewn together with brown thread.

"Did you hear anything about the type of weapon used?"

"Dr. Jones called in her report this morning. His heart stopped obviously, but the thing that stopped it was some kind of bolt."

"Yes, Chief Inspector Ainslie told me."

"They use bolt guns with animals, so the farming community might have some ideas. Ainslie put some guys onto it this morning. But he could also have been stabbed."

"It would have taken a lot of force to stab him with a bolt."

"I would think so. We haven't found the weapon yet, so we can't narrow things down."

They turned off the country road and into the overgrown driveway that led up to the big house. A policeman was standing at the front door, but apart from that, nothing suggested anything untoward had happened. Annabelle didn't get out of the car immediately.

"Jim, what do you know about Sergeant Lawrence? The lady police officer."

"Don't know much about her at all, to be honest. Decent officer. I mostly only hear the gossip from the Truro station. I get the impression she likes Inspector Nicholls. Not sure about his thoughts exactly, though she's more his type than Shenae in the canteen, who *definitely* likes him. Why do you ask?" Jim wasn't always the most tactful, or maybe the gossip about Annabelle and the inspector hadn't reached him.

"Oh, nothing, nothing at all." Annabelle waved away further discussion. "Let's get this done, shall we?"

Raven got out of the car and nodded to the policeman standing at the entrance to the house. "The reverend's just coming to pick something up that she left here last night," he rumbled in a low voice. Annabelle looked around her, surveying the horizon, unwilling to catch the policeman's eye amidst being party to an untruth. The police officer scrutinised Annabelle's clerical collar and waved them through. There was no sign of anyone inside.

"Follow me, Vicar."

Raven walked up the enormous stone stairway that led from the entry hall. They turned left when they reached the landing, and in silence, the pair walked down corridor after corridor until they reached a room that stood at the furthest point from the front door. Yellow police tape crisscrossed the entrance to the room. Raven held his finger to his lips as he reached for the doorknob. "This is the victim's bedroom," he whispered. He lifted the tape for Annabelle to duck under. "Be prepared."

The room was dark. The old, dusty, navy-blue curtains that covered the tall floor-to-ceiling windows and were thread through with silver were closed. Only a sliver of light escaped between the two curtains. It illuminated the room, providing a spotlight of glare for the dust floating through the thick air. There was just enough light to see what was there. It sent a chill through Annabelle as she looked around.

"Whoa," Annabelle exclaimed in a whisper the moment she stepped inside the room. Raven tried the light switch. It didn't work.

Like Sally's room, this one was large, with high ceilings and a picture rail that ran all around the walls. But where the ceiling of Sally's room was covered with ornamental plaster, here overhead was a fresco of chubby angel babies and their voluptuous mothers. Earthy colours combined with pale pink and blue to depict a soft, pleasing visual feast. Mothers and cherubs relaxed and played atop clouds set against a sky as blue as Annabelle's eyes. Whilst the fresco was faded, there was no doubting the artist's skill. The faces of the figures were exquisitely drawn.

But it was the rest of the room that caused Annabelle alarm. The heavenly scene began and ended above her, the delightful overhead backdrop only serving to throw the rest of the bedroom into stark relief. Annabelle stood still, her eyes roaming as she sought to determine what it could possibly mean.

Against one wall stood a rumpled bed covered by a bright red flag streaked with mud. In the centre of the flag was a black swastika inside a white circle. A pair of battered lace-up boots lay on the floor.

Above the bed, two crossed scythes, dusty and tarnished but threatening nonetheless, were held up by nails driven directly into the plaster. On either side, shadow boxes containing Nazi memorabilia hung from the picture rail. Annabelle looked closely and saw medals, pins, and uniform insignia. They were pinned to the backing like grotesque insects in which no one except the collector is interested.

Above the scythes were three dusty pistols, one above the other. Another antique gun lay on an old, upturned leather chest. Recruitment posters for Hitler Youth were stuck on the walls, whilst another Nazi flag lay draped artfully over a leather armchair. Raven picked up a large book and flicked through it.

"What is it?" Annabelle asked.

"Looks like a book of German Third Reich stamps."

"Not your regular collector, then?"

The room appeared ransacked. Drawers had been emptied, clothing strewn across the floor. A chest had been upturned and a photograph lay on the ground, the glass frame smashed. The picture was an old black and white, a photo of a man Annabelle didn't recognise. He had a sharp, short-back-and-sides haircut slicked with oil and a stern, thin-lipped expression.

"We should get out of here," Raven said. Annabelle continued to stare.

"This is all very strange," she said eventually. "I can't quite reconcile this scene with the person I met."

"Seems like he had a secret life, doesn't it?"

"It does look that way, Jim." Annabelle fingered the Nazi flag laying on the chair. It was flimsy, thin, threadbare in places. "Indeed it does."

"I thought we should follow this angle up, but the chief

discounted it. 'Bit of a hobby' was how Ainslie put it." Jim sniffed and pursed his lips. "I tried to get Sergeant Lawrence interested, but she wasn't concerned either. What do you think, Reverend?"

Annabelle continued to look around the room. On a dresser stood a mirror alongside a small box marked with Nazi symbols. Inside were seven ivory-handled razors, each one engraved with a day of the week. Annabelle took one of the razors out of the box and opened it. She held it up to the light. It was shiny, bright, and sharp. The sunlight piercing the room from between the gap in the curtains caught the blade's edge, blinding her momentarily. She shuddered and gently closed it before placing it back in the box and closing the lid.

Annabelle turned to face Jim, finally giving him all her attention. "I think, Constable Raven, that I am very thirsty and that I should go and seek a cup of hot tea. I will go downstairs to the kitchen to see if I can find someone who will join me, and over our tea, we can have a nice little chat about . . . *things,* if you get my drift."

"Yes, Ma'am, I mean, Reverend," Jim said, puffing out his chest. He almost saluted, delighted to have his concerns validated. "But now we should leave. It's more than my job's worth for you to be found here. Allow me." He raised the caution tape again. Annabelle slipped underneath it into the hallway, and with a quick look around, Constable Raven did the same.

CHAPTER SIXTEEN

ANNABELLE LOOKED UP as she rose from bobbing under the caution tape, her eyes shifting to the end of the landing. She got the distinct impression that someone was there, ducking out of sight. She ran to the corner but saw nothing down the long corridor that led away from her.

"Are you alright, Vicar? Would you like me to wait for you?" PC Raven asked her, running up.

"No, Jim, you be on your way. I'll get a lift into the village from someone, or I'll walk. I've no idea how long this will take. No need to make you wait. And it'll be better if I'm on my own. I'll be less conspicuous."

Jim looked at Annabelle, several inches taller than he, with her flowing cassock and clerical collar, her brown, chin-length hair, and bright, blue eyes that sparkled with intelligence. "I don't think you could be inconspicuous if you tried, Reverend. Are you sure? If we're right and there's more to this murder than meets the eye, you could be sharing your tea with a killer!" He whispered his last few words.

Annabelle waved his concerns away. "Nonsense, I'll be fine. I can't be putting people at ease with a uniformed bodyguard at my shoulder, can I? I'll call you if I get stuck."

"Well, if you're sure," Jim said, concern flooding his face.

"I'm sure, off you go." Annabelle made her way back through the house to the courtyard. It was early afternoon, and the sun was just past its peak. She could feel the heat on her back as she walked over to the doors that led into the kitchen. Before she opened them, she peered through.

Barnaby was hopping around the table. Behind him, Julia was at the sink filling the kettle. Annabelle knocked on the windowpane. Julia turned and waved her in. She seemed quite cheery.

"Hello, Vicar. Would you like a cup of tea? I was just going to make one."

"I'd love one, Julia. Thank you. How are things with you? Have you recovered from last night?"

"I was sorry to hear about Theo even though I wasn't his biggest fan. The idea that he was murdered is terrible. I spent the morning sitting with the others. Suki and Sally are in a dreadful state. I sent them outside to pick berries to distract them and keep them busy. Sally's father is in custody down the police station, did you hear?"

"I did. Seems plausible but very sad for Sally. What do you think? Could it be he who was responsible? That he is the murderer?"

"I don't know, but he had good reason to be angry with Theo."

"How so?"

Julia came over and put two mugs and a teapot on the table. She poured the tea. "We don't drink cow's milk here.

But we have some oat milk. Would you like that in your tea?"

"Um, yes. Why not?"

"Do you take sugar?"

"No, thank you."

Julia passed a mug over. Annabelle sipped her tea and squelched a wince. Tea wasn't quite the same with oat milk.

"Sally was in love with Theo," Julia said.

"Yes, she told me last night."

"She never said as much, not to us anyway, but you could tell from the way she looked at him. I'm pretty sure he played on it too. He didn't reciprocate, but he led her on. Let her believe there might be a chance. Theo wasn't a very nice person at times."

"And you think her father knew this? That Theo was leading her on?"

"I suspect so. He was young once, wasn't he? He probably recognised the signs. Sally's infatuation made her vulnerable, and I think her father's fears were very real and justified. Sally would have done whatever Theo wanted. She, of course, can't see any of this. I tried to tell her, but you saw how she was with him. Completely infatuated, I tell you."

"Having your father show up unannounced and demand you return home with him is hardly the way to win the heart and mind of a grown woman. She was in a no-win situation."

Julia acknowledged Annabelle's point over the rim of her mug. They heard female voices floating down the hall outside the kitchen. Suki and Sally, both of them carrying a basket of fruit, talked in low voices before appearing at the door. Suki had strawberries, Sally a basket of plums.

"Hi Vicar," Suki said, softly pressing her lips together.

"Hello," Annabelle said. "How are you today?" Both women looked exhausted, their youth and beauty hidden behind clouds of grief. Purple half-moons lay beneath their eyes, and their hair was disheveled. Sally's eyes were red and swollen. Her nose, too.

"Would you like some tea?" Julia asked them. "I can make you chamomile or peppermint. They will help."

Suki's reply was negative, but Sally responded. "Mint would be lovely. Thanks, Julia."

Sally slumped in a chair at the table and put her hands to her face. She sat silently as Julia bustled around, filling the kettle again and taking a teabag from a tin in a cupboard. Suki took the fruit to the sink and started to wash it under a running tap. A heavy, brooding, sorrowful atmosphere hung over the room like a toxic cloud. Annabelle leant over and rubbed Sally's back, and beneath her hands, Sally's face crumpled as she started to sob silently.

"There, there," Annabelle cooed. Julia brought over the tea and returned to the sink where Suki had abandoned the berries to sit on the steps in the sun.

"How am I going to go on without him?" Sally moaned.

"You'll find a way," Annabelle said. "One always does, in time."

Sally reached over and pulled a tissue out of a box. She wiped her face and blew her nose.

"He didn't love me, you know. Theo. He told me so. He was beautiful and charming and kind and loving. But he could be very cruel. He treated me as though I was some kind of irritant after I told him my feelings for him. Once, he . . . he actually pushed me! I couldn't understand it. He was so nice at first. I thought there was the possibility of a future between us. But he just turned cold. Then, that scene with my dad." Sally rolled her eyes and looked up at the ceiling. "Dad always was a hothead. He loves me but just doesn't know when to stop. He's always interfered in my life, telling me what to do, who to hang with. I have never seemed to be able to cut the ties completely. One of the reasons I joined the brotherhood was to get away from his overbearing ways. But he just followed me, didn't he?"

Annabelle patted her arm. "Fathers sometimes take a long time to accept that their little girls are all grown up."

"It was certainly a struggle for my dad. And now look where that's got him."

"Had he turned up here before?"

"Last night was the first time, but he's been harassing me and others in the group for a few months now. Letters and phone calls. He started soon after I joined. I hoped, after we moved from up north, he'd leave me alone." She looked wildly at Annabelle, fear in her eyes. "I should have done something! Stopped him somehow. Perhaps Theo would still be alive if I had. Oh, it's all my fault!" She started to cry again.

"Shush, shush, now," Annabelle said. "Theo and your father were on a collision course, and nothing you did or said would have changed the outcome."

Sally sobbed a little longer, finally wiping her eyes as she took big, shuddering breaths. Julia handed her tea over, and Sally sipped loudly.

"Why don't you go to bed for a nap?" Julia said. "You look beside yourself."

"That's a good idea," Annabelle said. "You look all in. I think even if you go now, you'll sleep all the way until morning."

Sally put the warm mug to her forehead and closed her eyes. "It does sound like a good idea." Annabelle helped Sally up.

When they got to her bedroom, Sally detached herself from Annabelle and ran water into the sink in the corner of her room. She stared at herself in the mirror until steam began to rise. After soaking a flannel, she held the hot towel to her red, puffy face, pressing it gently into her eye sockets.

"Sally, did you ever go into Theo's room?" Annabelle was sitting on Sally's bed.

Sally dragged the cloth down her face, wiping her cheeks as she looked at Annabelle's reflection in the mirror above the sink. "No, he didn't allow anyone in there. Not even Suki. He got sick once, and she tried to take him some soup. He screamed and yelled at her to get out. I think he threw something at her."

"You're sure no one went in there?"

"Hmm, I don't think so . . . Perhaps his mother? I'm sure no one else." She finished wiping her face and dried her hands.

She sat on the bed next to Annabelle and bent to take off her shoes. When she straightened, she said, "You know, now I come to think about it, Theo could be a bully. He had some strange ways. Secretive."

"How so?"

"He would go off for hours on end. He never told us where he went and would refuse to answer if we asked. And he really didn't pull his weight in the brotherhood."

"And you didn't complain? There were no arguments?"

"I think some were a little resentful."

"Who, Sally? Who was resentful?"

"Well," Sally hesitated. "Julia and Scott. They used to

moan about him a bit, but I suppose after a while we just got used to it, to him." She let out a long sigh. "I'm exhausted."

Annabelle helped Sally into bed and drew the curtains. "Sleep tight. Don't let the bedbugs bite."

"Don't joke, Reverend. There's a very real possibility of bedbugs in a place like this."

CHAPTER SEVENTEEN

ANNABELLE MADE HER way back to the kitchen. As she walked down the hallway to the former servants' quarters, she met Thomas going in the opposite direction. He stopped at the door. He was carrying a tripod and had a camera slung over his shoulder.

"Hello, Thomas, how are you today? Headed out?"

"H–hello Vicar. Yes, thought I'd get away for a b–bit. It's like a graveyard in here. The policeman said we could go outside if we stay inside the grounds."

"Well, it's a lovely day for it. Have you seen Margaret at all? I'm wondering how she's doing?"

"I h–haven't seen her today, but then I rarely see her, to be honest. She stays in her room most of the time. I wouldn't expect t–today to be any different."

"She must have been close to Theo. Not every mother and adult son could live together like this."

"P–possibly, but they didn't seem so particularly. I mean, she isn't exactly the w–warm and fuzzy type, is she?"

"But still, she has to be devastated. Her only son dead."

Thomas shifted, anxious to be away, but his face softened. "P–perhaps she's holding it all in, Vicar?"

"Perhaps. Well, have a good time on your shoot, Thomas."

Annabelle followed the windowless passageway to the kitchen and found Julia still pottering about. She was rolling out pastry, her strong, veined arms working the dough with a heavy marble rolling pin.

"How's Sally doing?" Julia asked.

"I think she'll be better after a good sleep. What are you making?"

"Pie. Chickpeas and veggies. I'm going to freeze it though. No one feels much like eating. Would you like some tofu ice cream? I made some earlier. Should be just about ready."

Annabelle was pretty sure her efforts at being "good" would be secure for the time she stayed at this particular house. "I'm fine, thank you. Were you vegan before you came here?"

"Oh yes! I became a vegetarian when I was a girl after I learnt that my Sunday roast was formerly one of the gorgeous cows that lived in the field behind our house. I haven't eaten meat since. I stopped eating anything that came from an animal when I was at uni, so it has been years now." Julia gave Annabelle the determined look of one who has had to defend her choices many times. "I've seen how people treat animals. It is disgusting."

Julia carefully picked up the round of pastry with her rolling pin and draped it over the pie dish. She gently pushed the dough into the corners with her fingertips and reached into a drawer to fish out a fork, pricking the pie base to prevent it from rising in the oven. "When I moved in with the brotherhood, they still ate meat. I was horrified and made a commitment to veganism a condition of my joining. Theo was game, and I soon converted the others. It helped that I did all the cooking."

"Who was in the brotherhood when you joined?" Annabelle had reclaimed her mug of now-cold tea and cradled it between her hands as she sat at the table across from Julia.

"Theo and a couple of blokes who have since left. It was just the two of us for a while."

"Did you get to know him well?"

Julia paused pricking out her pastry crust. She looked up. "Oh no. I know he was abroad for a bit. Asia, Australia, I think. And he went to university somewhere, but on the whole, he didn't talk about himself much. After a few weeks, Thomas arrived, then Sally, and finally, Scott. Of course, Suki and Margaret came for the ride once we moved in here."

"So you're the longest-serving member now?"

"I suppose I am." Julia bent over to place the pie in the oven. In its day, the large kitchen would have contained an iron range, but now there was only a white freestanding stove that wobbled when Julia opened the door.

Julia stood up, pink from the rush of heat that had escaped from the oven. She wiped her hands on her apron. "Not that it means anything. We are a fluid community. People will come, people will go."

"What do you think will happen to the group now?"

"I really couldn't say. Theo was the key to having this house to live in, but I don't know who owns it. An uncle, I think. Without Theo here to fight for us, we may be cast out on our ear."

"It isn't Margaret's house then?"

"No. After her husband lost everything in the crash, I

believe they went from being very well off to almost desti- tute. Serves them right. Then he died, and she really was up a creek without a paddle. There's some rumours floating around that she has a wealthy brother, but he refused to help her, and she had to throw herself on Theo's mercy. She was here as Theo's guest. He extended the invitation for her to live here as a courtesy. What exactly Theo's arrangement was with the owner, I can't imagine."

"So what will you do? If you can't stay here, I mean."

"Roll on, I guess. Something will work out. I don't need very much, just somewhere to lay my head, a small job, and Barnaby, of course. I can't forget him. He goes everywhere with me." Annabelle looked at the rabbit. Barnaby had fetched up next to the warm teapot on the table and was dozing. Julia wiped her hands on a tea towel featuring the faded faces of a royal wedding couple. "Cooking in a vegan café might be fun. More tea, Vicar?"

"No, thank you. I should be going. I'm glad to see you're doing so well, and I hope Sally feels better after her sleep. I'll come back in a couple of days and see how you're all doing." Annabelle opened the doors to the courtyard and squeezed past Suki, who was still sitting on the steps.

"Are you off, Reverend?"

"Yes, I'm going to walk back to the village. It's a lovely day, and it shouldn't take me too long if I cut through Lolly Lane."

"I'll walk with you a way. I could do with the exercise. It's no fun being cooped up in the house, especially under the circumstances." Suki pushed herself up from the steps wearily.

"Of course. How is your mother holding up?" They walked across the courtyard and under an archway into the grounds.

"I haven't seen her today. She didn't answer when I knocked on her door, but that isn't unusual. She's a funny old bird, my mother."

"She seemed shocked last night, understandably. She was very composed but stunned, I thought."

"I think you're being kind. She was distant and aloof. Worse. She's jaded and cynical. She's been like that since Dad died. Actually, she's always been like it but more so since he passed away."

"Does she have any support? Any family to help her? Besides you?"

"Nope. It's just Mother and me now. All my grandparents are dead. Mum has a brother, but they don't speak. There's been lots of trouble in her family.

"Will you stay here, do you think?"

"I don't know. My uncle inherited all my grandparents' money *and* cut Mum out of his will, making Theo his beneficiary. He has no children of his own and is in a care home. This is his house. Theo persuaded him to let us use it. I've never met him, but Theo knew him well. Goodness knows what will happen now."

"So who will benefit from your uncle's will now that Theo is gone?"

"I don't know. Me, perhaps? But I have no contact with my uncle. He could have left his estate to a bunch of cats, for all I know."

They walked in silence until they reached the outer trees of the woods. "Look, I'm going to leave you here," Suki said. She looked back in the direction of the house. "I don't really want to go into the woods again so soon."

"Of course. I understand."

Suki hesitated. The two women stood awkwardly, each waiting for the other to make a move.

"If I can help with anything . . . ?" Annabelle said. She raised her eyebrows expectantly.

Suki gave her a strained smile. "No, there's nothing, Reverend. Thank you for coming by."

"Well, I'll be seeing you then." Annabelle turned to walk away.

"Actually, there is something, Annabelle, Reverend. Look, it's probably nothing." Suki paused. Annabelle waited.

Suki sighed. "It's just . . . well, Theo and Scott had a blazing row a couple of days ago. I went to the forge to see Scott, hang out with him for a bit, and there they were, going at it hammer and tongs."

After her initial hesitation, Suki's words rushed out, like water after a dam had broken. "It was over money. Scott was accusing Theo of stealing funds from the group, funds he wasn't distributing fairly, and not keeping proper records, so we couldn't trace what happened to it. Theo was furious. I've never seen him so angry. At one point, Scott grabbed him. Scott's a good earner for the group, and I think he feels under-appreciated."

Suki's shoulders sagged, and she looked down at the ground. She gently kicked a stone with her foot. "I can't believe he's a murderer, though. I didn't tell the police because I didn't want to get him into trouble. But perhaps you could talk to him? He seemed to like you when you were at dinner the other night. Scott can be a little uncommunicative at times. Surly. He doesn't like everyone. And perhaps he knows something. He's at the smithy if you want to see him."

"Thanks, Suki. You go back to the house and see how your mother is. I'm sure she could do with some company however she may appear."

The two women went their separate ways. Annabelle, after initially pressing on through the trees, changed her mind and walked out of them again. She decided to take a route that skirted the outside of the wood. It would take her much longer to get home, but it offered open skies, a clear view, and didn't entertain the darker corners of her imagination.

CHAPTER EIGHTEEN

ANNABELLE DECIDED TO leave talking to Scott for another day. She was eager to get home. At the junction with the main road, she eschewed the path tracked into the grass next to the hedgerow and, noticing the green public footpath sign that pointed across the fields, crossed the road to climb over the stile. Navigating it in her cassock wasn't easy, but after several attempts and much gathering of skirts, she managed it without snagging anything.

As she walked down the gentle slope into the village, her mind again turned to Mike. Just a couple of weekends ago, they'd walked this grassy path. It had been a hot, sunny day like this one, and the dogs had gambolled ahead. Mike and Annabelle had brought a picnic, and down at the river's edge, they'd spread their rug in the shade under trees that overhung the water.

It was a romantic spot, and Annabelle thought, hoped, that Mike might take their relationship to the next level with a kiss. Even some kind of declaration of intention would have been progress. But whilst there'd been lots of direct eye contact and the occasional touching of fingertips, it had been incidental and accidental and hadn't led to anything. She felt clouds of hopelessness descend and she felt uncharacteristically sorry for herself.

Annabelle looked about her at the glorious countryside and sighed. She pressed on, telling herself she had much to be grateful for and that "God works in mysterious ways," a truism she usually avoided in her work because she felt it hackneyed, supercilious, and unhelpful. She picked up a long, unusually straight brown stick. It would be perfect for staking the sunflower she had grown outside her kitchen window, but which was so bent over on itself that the yellow petals almost touched the ground. Annabelle put the stick in her belt and tightened the knot. "Come on, Bumble," she whispered, using the nickname her brother had coined for her. "Pull yourself together. Stiff upper lip and all that."

"There are three things to remember, Bumble," her mother had told her late one afternoon after a hard day cleaning other people's houses. "When times are tough, 'pull yourself together,' 'least said, soonest mended,' and 'mustn't grumble,' are the best pieces of advice. Don't forget them, and you won't go far wrong."

Annabelle smiled at the memory. Annabelle's parents were solid East London folk whose pride in their daughter's acceptance to Cambridge University was matched only by her graduation three years later. Her success had been extraordinary amongst her peers. Annabelle knew that she lived her dream of being a countryside rector largely because of her parent's sacrifices and the beliefs they had instilled in her, attitudes that still formed the basic fabric of traditional British life.

Annabelle looked ahead at the jumble of dwellings that rose from the middle of the rolling green and yellow fields that spread outwards as far as her eye could see. Upton St. Mary had been relatively untouched by modern development, and the view had remained virtually the same for centuries.

She studied the roofs of family homes and small businesses. Grey slate and tile covered the medium-sized and larger buildings whilst thatch protected the smaller cottages, the care of which generated a thriving business for Johnny Morton, the local thatcher. Inside every house, whether large and lavish or humble and homely, Annabelle knew good people lived there, genuine people, all deserving of respect, support, and an opportunity to thrive. She considered it her job to minister and take care of those people. She lifted her face to the sky. It was just that sometimes, it would be nice if someone could take care of *her*.

In the centre of the huddle of buildings was the soaring, majestic stone spire of St. Mary's. Annabelle was particularly fond of the yellow lichen that grew on the steeple's sides. It made the five-centuries-old spire appear to glow when the sun shone in the late afternoon, a sight she could see now as she made her way there.

Annabelle always fancied that the spire acted as an alternative compass for travellers, directing them to a place of care and comfort when they were away from home. She distracted herself from her thoughts of Mike, their stalled relationship, and the group in the big house by focusing on her church and the comfort and sense of belonging it gave her. She quickened her pace, suddenly wanting to be home already.

As she walked the last few yards to her whitewashed cottage, her pace slowed, however. She spied Constable Jim Raven and Philippa standing outside her garden gate.

Raven's hands were in his pockets. Philippa's arms were folded. A police car stood at the kerb.

"Here she is," Raven said. He looked fresh-faced, ruddy, much more cheerful than he had earlier.

"Finally. Annabelle, we've been looking for you *everywhere*." Philippa was flustered. Pink spots flushed her cheeks. Around her waist, she wore a brightly coloured apron printed with yellow dahlias. The fact that she was wearing it in public alarmed Annabelle. Philippa was meticulous about not wearing house garments outside. 'Pinnies' were for indoors.

"Is something wrong?"

Philippa took her by the arm and quickly guided her up the garden path. "I was doing the church accounts, and there was a knock at the door. You've got a visitor. That's why Constable Raven is here. He's *security*." Philippa raised her chin and straightened her back.

Annabelle stopped abruptly and took her arm from Philippa's grip "What do you mean, he's *security*?" Annabelle looked over her shoulder at Raven, who shrugged and raised his hands, palms up.

Philippa nodded briskly at the front door. "In the kitchen," she said, her eyebrows raised.

Leaving Philippa behind, Annabelle pushed open the front door and marched down the hall to her rustic, cosy kitchen. It was her favourite room. Exposed beams ran across the ceiling and down the walls. It was a place of calm, communion, and cupboards full of cake.

Annabelle entered to see a woman sitting at the table, a teapot, two cups and saucers, a milk jug, and a sugar bowl in front of her. At the sound of the opening door, Margaret Westmoreland slowly turned to Annabelle and looked her up and down.

After a day of corralling forty schoolchildren, a prowl through a dusty bedroom, a ramble among woodland, and an hour's hike through the hilly countryside, Annabelle was not looking her best. Her hair was fluffy and mussed, the hem of her cassock dusty, her face flushed from sun and exercise.

Margaret, in contrast, wore a black and white dress with a blue leaf and pink flower print. The sleeves were sheer. Around her neck, she wore a single string of pearls, and a matching bracelet on her wrist. Her hair was freshly styled, and she wore a full face of makeup, her lipstick matching the pink of her dress exactly. She existed in a haze of floral scent.

"Margaret! So good to see you!" Annabelle's arms swung back and forth, and she was immediately conscious of behaving like an awkward schoolgirl. She clamped her mouth shut, cupping her elbow in one hand, the other covering her chin and lips so she didn't say anything more. She looked steadily at Margaret before pulling out a chair to sit down.

"Oof." Annabelle doubled over as the stick in her belt jabbed her in the ribs. "Sorry, sorry. Forgot it was there." She stood to open the back door, and pulling the stick from her waist like a sword, she threw it outside without taking her eyes off her visitor. With her foot, she kicked the door shut and plopped down on her chair, lifting the teapot and immediately pouring herself a cup. "Now, where were we?"

Margaret stared at her. "I hope I haven't made a mistake," she said. "It took some convincing to get permission from that ghastly police sergeant to come here."

"Ah, that's why you've got *security*?"

"What?"

"Constable Raven. He's here to escort you."

"I told them, as the mother of the murder victim, I needed some spiritual support."

"Ah, I see." Annabelle put her cup down and dipped her chin, focusing her gaze on Margaret as she looked at her from under her eyelashes.

"Except that's not why I'm here, at all."

CHAPTER NINETEEN

"I HEARD YOU at the house earlier, talking to the others. I saw you coming out of Theo's room. I wanted . . . to explain." For the first time, Margaret Westmoreland looked vulnerable. She blinked rapidly. Her eyes were moist.

Annabelle's heartbeat slowed, and her shoulders relaxed. "Please, Margaret, go ahead. Take all the time you need." She reached over and placed a box of tissues within Margaret's reach.

The older woman took one and blew on it delicately. "You see, Reverend, I loved my son very much. He was charming and kind. He was smart and such a cheeky little chap when he was young." She smiled at her memories, focusing on a point behind Annabelle's head. The older woman gave a little sniff and dabbed her upper lip. "But he could also be cruel and selfish. There's a strong streak of spitefulness and malice in my family, and Theo didn't escape its curse."

Margaret looked out of the window directly ahead of

her, but now she focused her gaze on Annabelle. "Reverend, it pains me to say this, but I was ashamed of my son. I know that sounds terrible, but I was, I am. Oh, I know I might come across as one of those frightful women who care only about appearances, but I'm not, in fact, one of them. I have wondered over and over if I had anything to do with Theo's . . . problems, or if I could have done anything about them had I known earlier."

"What problems were they, Margaret?" Annabelle asked. She handed over another tissue. Margaret wiped her eyes, her tea long forgotten.

"I have an uncle, you see. We haven't spoken in years. He has no family, and as his closest relative, I was his heir before he disinherited me."

"Over what?"

"I can't even remember now, any number of things. It doesn't matter. He was an all-round nasty piece of work." Margaret again looked over Annabelle's shoulder, lost in thought before remembering herself. She shook her head. "My uncle is Lord Drummond." She paused, but seeing no recognition on Annabelle's expression, Margaret continued. "In his prime, he was a friend to the stars, politicians, aristo-crats. He was named in a political scandal in 1982 that brought down half the Cabinet. But he started out as simple Alexander Drumrof, a poor German refugee who made his way to England as a teenager along with the rest of my family just before the breakout of World War II. After they anglicised their name to Drummond, Alexander made a pile of money in arms dealing. Later, he received a title for *services* to the country and dished out favours to the rich and famous. He did it for years and profited handsomely. He lived in splendour in Kensington, only moving down here a decade or so ago. After my husband died and we lost everything, I appealed to Alexander for help. I begged, Reverend. Can you imagine how humiliating that was for me?" Margaret's voice was thick. Annabelle leant over to hold her hand.

"He refused to help us, so I begged a little more. The more he refused, the more I begged. In the end, we came to . . . a deal." She gulped. "He offered to educate Theo at a private boarding school. He'd settle a small trust on him for day-to-day expenses and make him his heir." Margaret took her hand from Annabelle's and rubbed her brow. She stared down at the table.

"That doesn't seem so bad. What was the problem?"

"It was what he wanted in return. He wanted Theo to live with him during the school holidays. We weren't to see him regularly, just the occasional weekend. I would oversee Theo's trust fund until he was eighteen, which meant that if I were careful, I could use it to live on. But Alexander became Theo's de facto parent."

"I see. That is very cruel." Annabelle's eyes were full of pity for the woman although she couldn't help wondering why, to support herself and keep custody of her son, she hadn't simply gone out to work. The price of charity seemed terribly high.

"But that wasn't all."

"Oh?"

"If I'd thought Alex would have been a good influence on Theo, I wouldn't have been too concerned. I realise that must sound terribly callous, but people of my class are different from yours, Reverend." Annabelle drew herself up, preparing for an insult that Margaret's condescension implied would be forthcoming.

"People like me regularly give our children away to those who we believe will develop them, give them character, prepare them for the destiny we believe is theirs. Cosy family mealtimes and mother and son outings are secondary to other priorities. No, it wasn't that Theo would be going away. It was what he was going away to do."

"And what was that, Margaret?" Annabelle was now utterly confused by all the twists this story was taking.

"Alexander was going to brainwash him," Margaret said baldly.

Annabelle stared at her. "Really? How?"

"He was planning to indoctrinate him in his political beliefs. Despite all he owed England, despite how he paid homage to the freedoms and privileges he benefitted from, my uncle was a Nazi sympathiser. He has been his entire life. He's 93 now.

"All this Lord Darthamort nonsense was Alexander's doing. It was he who taught Theo about exploiting people. Alexander told him that most people are sheep crying out to be herded and that Theo would be doing them a favour if he became their leader. Clearly, Alexander was right, at least in part, because Theo had no trouble getting people to believe in him. It was Alexander who created this whole charade about Petrie and Darthamort. Theo simply lived it out and got others to live it too.

"Reverend, my son came to believe that kindness, decency, and honour were akin to weakness. He despised other people. Theo saw them as tools to exact a better situation for himself, and he took pleasure in using them. I heard that Richard Venables called Theo a psychopath. I would agree with him."

Annabelle took a sip of her tea. It was cold, but she hardly noticed. "You heard about that?"

Margaret turned down the corners of her mouth. "Suki told me. When Theo was a child, Alexander sought to mold him in his likeness. I don't know exactly how he did it, but Theo, on the occasions we would see him, changed from the boy we knew. He was darker, more brooding. His personality changed completely. He would take long walks alone in the countryside. He started hunting, something in which he'd shown no interest before. He would lambast us with far-right, Aryan-state, anti-semitic, nationalist politics. We didn't know what to do. Eventually, Theo turned eighteen and decided to go to university abroad. We supported that. We hoped that if Theo was away from the toxic environment created by Alexander, he might come around. But when he finally came home after graduating and spending some years flitting about the world, it seemed he hadn't changed one bit."

"That's a shame."

"But he had learnt to hide his nature better. In some ways, that was worse. Now he appeared to be the Theo we had known as a young boy, but there was a hateful personality lurking just under the surface."

"Did you know about his room?"

"Yes, he didn't hide it from me. I was beholden to him, dependent. I was probably the only person he was truthful with, and I kept his secrets, to my shame."

There was silence for a moment. Annabelle considered the question she felt compelled to ask. "Were you ashamed enough to kill him?"

"My own son? Don't be ridiculous. Why would I do that?"

"For shame."

"I wouldn't kill him. I may be pathetic, but I'm not depraved, even if he was. Besides, he was my meal ticket."

"How did you support yourself once Theo was eighteen?"

"During the years I controlled his trust fund, I'd invested a little. We lived off that. It was hardly anything, but the markets were slowly recovering. It wasn't enough though, and we ended up here." Margaret breathed out through her nose and drummed her fingertips on the table. "Look, I'm not proud of my circumstances, Reverend. I know who, and what I am. I was born into money, gained more through marriage, then lost it all. In the process, I ruined relationships, never worked, and drank too much. I am totally useless and ill-suited to poverty. My son is, was, more pragmatic, less burdened, and could bend with the wind. He was clever. He could make honey from milk. I needed him.

"Other people adored him. He could wind them around his little finger. Women were always falling in love with him. Sally is only the latest in a very long string of girls. But he never cared for any of them. He was only in love with himself. My sticking with him might not have been honourable, but it was expedient. And it kept me in gin."

"Do you not have any other family you could turn to? Besides Suki?"

"No. Suki is as useless as I am at the practical things in life, but at least she has a sunnier disposition. She's young and beautiful. Someone will marry her, and she'll be alright. She'll probably inherit my brother's estate now that Theo is gone, although I suspect that she'll burn her way through it in unfortunate haste."

"So Suki has a motive for killing her brother. Could she have killed him?"

"Good grief, no. Suki couldn't roast a chicken let alone shoot a person, especially her own brother. What kind of people do you take us for?"

"Then what about a spurned lover, one of those girls you mention?"

"It's possible, but I doubt it. They always tended to be easily impressionable, vulnerable girls. Ones who would fall for his tales."

"And so what was your exact purpose for coming here today? To tell me all this, if it wasn't to expunge your soul?"

"That wasn't it. I'm way beyond redemption, Reverend. I know that. If I'd had more courage or been a better mother, none of this would have happened. The reason I'm talking to you is to tell you about Thomas. The police seem pretty stuck on this Richard Venables, but I've seen you snooping around, and I think you should look at Thomas."

"Thomas? What about him?" Annabelle was surprised. After Margaret's tale of depravity, talk of mild, gentle Thomas was startling.

"Thomas is a Jew. His mother, the one he thinks no one knows about, survived the concentration camps. She was just nine when she was liberated, an orphan. I visited Alexander one day; his care home is just a few miles away. I hoped I could get him to change his mind about his estate and leave me at least a little in his will when he died."

"And did he?"

"Did he what?"

"Change his mind and leave you something?"

"No, I left it too late to ask. He was beyond reason. But I did see a name on a bedroom door that intrigued me. *Eta Reisman*. When I got back to the house, I asked Thomas about her because they shared such an unusual last name. He confirmed that she was his mother. He told me not to tell the others. I looked her up in the Holocaust database, she was her family's sole survivor. They were members of the Resistance in Belgium—her father forged papers. Eventually, though, they were shipped off to Buchenwald. It's true," Margaret said. "Look her up."

"And you think Thomas may have known about Theo's Nazi sympathies and harboured a grudge?"

"Well, wouldn't you?"

CHAPTER TWENTY

PHILIPPA FUMED AS she vacuumed the living room carpet, her mouth pressed into a tight moue. Yesterday she'd discreetly applied herself to some gardening whilst Margaret Westmoreland talked to Annabelle, but now Philippa had returned to complete her chores in the house. The church accounts lay forgotten on the dining table, files and loose papers piled meticulously in accordance with a system known only to Philippa as she pushed the vacuum back and forth with such vehemence that it was surprising she didn't destroy any furniture.

Annabelle viewed the ferocity with which her housekeeper and church secretary was flying around the room and silently wondered if the vacuum was Philippa's version of a broomstick, before chastising herself for such an uncharitable thought. Annabelle was the reason for Philippa's bad mood. When Margaret Westmoreland had left the cottage, accompanied by PC Raven, Philippa had knocked on the back door. Annabelle was sitting at the kitchen table, papers in front of her, a pen in her hand.

"Coo-ee Annabelle! Is it alright if I come in?"

"Yes, yes, the coast is clear."

"I was getting on with the accounts when that woman arrived, but shall I put the kettle on?"

"Gosh, I'm fine, Philippa. Really. I've had so much tea today, I'm going to drown if I have any more."

"What about a scone, then? I've made some fresh."

"No thanks. You know I'm trying to be good."

"What are you doing?" Philippa was hovering.

"I'm setting out the program for the show. Working on the cast list. Woe betide me if I leave anyone out. Parents will have my guts for garters." Annabelle didn't lift her eyes from the list she was working on.

Philippa slapped her thighs and looked about her. She opened a cupboard and brought out a cylindrical tub, taking off the lid and waving it under Annabelle's nose.

"Chocolate Hobnob?"

Annabelle recoiled. "No, Philippa. I told you, I'm trying to be good. Anyone would think you didn't want me to lose a bit of weight. Wasn't it you telling me a while back that I should?"

Philippa ignored Annabelle's question because it was true. She rapped the tube of Hobnobs on the table's wooden surface, pulling out a chair and sitting down with a plop. She stared at the vicar.

Annabelle sighed and put her pen down wearily. "What is it, Philippa?"

"Oh, nothing." Philippa picked up a napkin from a pile that lay on the tabletop. She started rolling it into a tube.

"Philippa? This wouldn't have anything to do with the visitor I just had, would it? The one who brought her own *security*?"

"Well, I was wondering what business she had here. She lives up with that cult. She could, for all we know, be a murderer. And she is, after all, a *vegan*." Philippa didn't look up from her rolling. The freshly ironed and starched napkin now curled at the corners.

"I'm not at liberty to divulge our conversation, Philippa. I'm sorry."

"But Reverend, there's a murderer on the loose."

"The police have someone in custody. And besides, if I have information relevant to the inquiry, the place to share it is with the appropriate authorities." Annabelle was being officious on purpose. She knew Philippa was fishing for gossip.

"Well, I think you should share it with us, Annabelle. The villagers could be in danger!"

"I really don't think that's the case, Philippa. Now, if you don't mind, I need to get on with this list. I'm missing two names." Annabelle dropped her head and started examining the paper in front of her.

"Right. Well. I'll be off home then. I'll see you in the morning."

Abruptly, Philippa stood up and with an injured air swept out of the room, leaving the tube of Hobnobs on the table. Annabelle looked up and with a roll of her eyes, pushed them out of arms reach.

Now, as she stood at the doorway to the living room watching Philippa wield the vacuum like it was a weapon, Annabelle considered that perhaps she should share Margaret's information, at least with the police. Her conversation with Theo's mother had weighed on her overnight. She felt she was breaking a confidence. She wrestled with the idea of betraying Thomas, but Margaret's news was pertinent, and Annabelle felt she had a duty to tell the police what she knew.

"I'm going down the station, Philippa." Philippa gave no

reply. Annabelle really was in the doghouse. There was a rap at the door. Annabelle answered it.

"Oh, hello, Vicar!" It was Barbara. She was wearing a violet and gold dress with matching eye makeup.

"Hello, Barbara, what can I do for you?"

"Well, um, I need to speak to Philippa. I heard her vacuuming so I thought I'd drop by."

"Come on in. I'm just on my way out."

"Oh good, um, going anywhere nice?"

"Just the police station. See you later." Annabelle stood back to let Barbara by, the pub owner's strong perfume tickling her nose as she wafted past. Halfway down the garden path, Annabelle patted her pockets, then rummaged in her bag. She'd left her phone inside the house. Turning, Annabelle made her way back to the cottage. As she opened the front door, she heard Barbara and Philippa talking in the living room.

"We can Google him, Barbara."

"Google? That can't be right, Philippa. You're thinking of goggle box, surely?"

"I'm not, Barbara. Google, as in googly eyes. Like the reverend when the inspector is around. Googly."

Annabelle closed her eyes. She picked up her phone from the hall table and shut the front door quietly.

"Good morning, Mr. Penrose!" she called out as the elderly man walked his grey pitbull, Kylie, along the lane just as he had every morning for years, long before Annabelle arrived in the village.

Mr. Penrose raised his walking stick in salute. "Lovely morning for it, Vicar." Annabelle sneezed, Barbara's perfume having finally overwhelmed her.

A few minutes later, Annabelle pulled her Mini Cooper into a parking space outside the police station. She quickly ran up the steps into the old building. Behind reception stood a familiar face, Constable McAllister, Upton St. Mary's only female police officer.

"Hello, Reverend. We don't see you in here very often."

"No, thank goodness," Annabelle smiled. She'd always liked Jenny McAllister. The woman was friendly and efficient, and Annabelle suspected the station wouldn't operate nearly as well without her. "I wonder if Chief Inspector Ainslie is in."

"He's not, I'm afraid. But Sergeant Lawrence is here. Would you like to see her?"

"Oh, um . . ." Annabelle didn't want to see the slim, spiky sergeant with the sharp haircut but couldn't put her finger on exactly why. "Yes, that would be lovely, thank you."

PC McAllister disappeared but returned shortly. "She'll be with you momentarily."

"Thanks, Jenny."

The desk phone rang, and the constable reached for the receiver. "Upton St. Mary Police."

The police station reception was small and Annabelle, not expecting to wait long and not wishing to intrude, turned to examine the police noticeboard with unswerving dedication. After seven minutes, she sat down. After another seven, she got out her phone and started scrolling aimlessly. Five minutes after that, she started to read a recent police report about the capture of a swan found wandering along the M5 near Exeter.

Eventually, Sergeant Lawrence appeared. She opened the door to the back office with force. "Morning," she barked. "Sorry to keep you waiting." Annabelle didn't get the impression that the sergeant was sorry at all, but she stood to follow the woman. The officer was dressed as before in black combat pants, a black t-shirt, and this time, a vest more suited to the streets of New York than Upton St. Mary.

"Gosh, a bullet-proof vest in our little village," Annabelle said, laughing a little longer than was appropriate.

Lawrence looked down at what she was wearing. "Not bullet-proof, stab-proof," she said.

"Oh, right."

"So, what can I do you for? Is it about the murder investigation?" Sergeant Lawrence sat back in her chair. She didn't look at Annabelle but at her computer screen, her arms stretched out, fingers poised over the keyboard.

"Yes, I received some information yesterday. From Margaret Westmoreland. I thought you should hear it." Annabelle spent the next few minutes relaying what Margaret had told her about her family history, Theo's fascination with Nazis, the Lord Darthamort connection, Thomas' mother being a Holocaust survivor, and Margaret's opinion that Theo was a nasty piece of work. Annabelle omitted telling Sergeant Lawrence about her own visit to Theo's room. She didn't want to get PC Raven into trouble.

Sergeant Lawrence typed all of this into her computer. "Why are you telling me this?"

Annabelle was surprised. "Because I thought it relevant to the investigation, Sergeant. There are several lines of inquiry I thought you might be interested in following up."

Sergeant Lawrence typed furiously, finishing with a final thump as she finished her sentence before flicking a switch. Her screen went dark. She swivelled in her chair and leant her forearm on her desk. She stared at Annabelle intently.

"Thank you for coming in today to tell us this. We will

review your information and take action if we think it necessary." Lawrence reached for her phone, effectively dismissing Annabelle.

"Necessary? But of course, it's necessary. At the very least, you should speak to Thomas about his mother."

Lawrence didn't look up from her phone. "We have someone in custody. We're just waiting for forensics before we file charges. We are quite sure we have our man."

"But, but . . . There hasn't been a thorough investigation. You're making your facts fit your theory."

The woman looked up. "Is that so? Learnt police investigative procedure from Inspector Nicholls, did you?"

Annabelle went pink. "I–I don't see how that's relevant."

"He talks about you down at the station in Truro. Seems to think a lot of you." Sergeant Lawrence muttered something under her breath that Annabelle didn't quite catch. There was a bang as a door was roughly pushed open. The bulk of Chief Inspector Ainslie appeared in the doorframe, blocking out the light that would otherwise have streamed in from the brightly lit reception.

"What's going on, Scar— Ah, Vicar. What are you doing here?"

"Miss Dixon came to give us some information about the murder investigation, sir," Sergeant Lawrence said. "I've logged it all. She was just leaving."

"I see. Well, thank you for coming in," Ainslie said. "We'll be in touch if we need to speak to you again." Lawrence looked sharply at Annabelle. Annabelle stood but hesitated. "You can run along home now." Ainslie's gaze hardened, and he leant in. "Let us professionals handle this investigation. We know what we're doing."

Annabelle's eyes closed halfway. The pink spots on her

cheeks got pinker. "Well then, I shall leave you to it." She walked, her chin high, to the door before turning. "And by the way," Lawrence and Ainslie looked at her in surprise, "it's *Reverend* Dixon." She spun on her heel and left the station, almost forgetting to acknowledge Jenny as she passed. She climbed in her car, strapped herself in, and blew out her cheeks. A small smile crossed her face. *He talks about you down at the station.*

As she looked over her shoulder to reverse her Mini out of the parking space, she noticed a familiar figure push against the doors of the station. The man squinted. It was the first time in nearly two days that Richard Venables had seen daylight. He looked disheveled and unshaven. There were bags under his eyes. Deep lines on his face made him look older than he had just a couple of days earlier. He shrugged on a bomber jacket and quickly tripped down the steps. He turned in the direction of the High Street, passing villagers walking in the opposite direction. No one but Annabelle paid him any heed.

CHAPTER TWENTY-ONE

ANNABELLE WAS HAVING a hard time concentrating. She was writing her notes for Sunday's sermon. A few words would come, but then her eyes would stray to the garden outside. For a while, she sat mesmerised by the sight of her bees. They methodically flew back and forth from their two hives. If only life were so orderly. She got up and poured a glass of water, drinking it over the kitchen sink, simultaneously waving to Mr. Penrose, who was now taking Kylie for her afternoon walkies.

Annabelle turned and sighed, flopping back down on her seat at the table. She picked up her pen and bent over, ready to start writing again, only to be interrupted by Biscuit jumping onto her lap. It was an action so rare that Annabelle put down her pen to stroke the cat's cheeks and look deep into her eyes, "You're not sickening for something are you, Biscuit?"

Biscuit purred and forcefully pushed her head under Annabelle's hand. With her paw, she prodded the pen out of Annabelle's reach. "Okay, okay." With one hand,

Annabelle scratched Biscuit's ears, with the other she began tapping out a text to Mike.

```
Venables was released. What do you think
that means?
```

Annabelle waited to see if she would get a response, rubbing Biscuit's ears between her thumb and forefinger as she waited. There was a ping, and she picked up her phone eagerly.

```
They can't have enough evidence, and
they've run out of time. No choice but to
let him go.
```

```
Do you think I should speak to him?
```

```
To Venables? Leave it to Ainslie. There's a
maniac out there, and until he's caught,
you could be in danger.
```

```
But I might be able to find something out
they can't.
```

```
Seriously, Annabelle, leave it to the
police. They're the professionals.
```

A little stung by Mike's last text, Annabelle didn't reply. She buried her nose in Biscuit's fur and then lay her cheek on her silky, soft coat, enjoying the feel of it against her skin.

There was a rustle, and Philippa, once more wearing the dahlia-patterned pinny, starched to a standard that would make a sergeant-major smile, appeared in the doorway, duster in hand.

"Venables has been released," Annabelle said simply. Philippa gasped with horror.

"No! A murderer is on the loose! I told you!"

"Calm down, Philippa. Mike says they wouldn't have let him go if they had evidence."

"But still, either way, there's a murderer on the loose." Philippa started to pace the kitchen floor, wringing her hands. "I must tell people, warn the village!"

"Mike says I should stay out of it."

"And he's right! You could be in danger if you go blundering in!"

Annabelle blinked at Philippa's retort. Respect for her detecting skills clearly wasn't in evidence amongst those who knew her best.

She heard a clacking on the path and looked out to see Barbara hastening through the gate and up the garden path. There was a smart tap at the door.

"Back again, Barbara?"

"That man, the one I barred, the one they arrested for the murder up at the big house, he's out. I saw him at lunchtime as he left the newsagents," Barbara said before she'd even set foot over the threshold. "Want me to speak to him? Get him to talk to you?"

"Don't encourage her, Barbara!" Philippa said marching over to Annabelle's side.

"Oh yes!" Annabelle replied, her eyes bright. Seeing Philippa fuming, she quickly rephrased her reply. "Hmm, that might be helpful," she said in a low voice. Philippa huffed and looked mutinously at Barbara.

"I'll get him in the pub, Reverend. I'll text you," Barbara said, ignoring Philippa.

"I thought you barred him from your pub," Philippa said.

"If he's going to be in one of the pubs, and he surely will be, it might as well be mine. That way, I can keep an eye on him."

Annabelle smiled. Barbara was a matriarchal figure like no other, and the village would be much the worse without her.

"Right you are, Barbara!" Annabelle was suddenly full of energy and enthusiasm. "Synchronise watches! I'll wait for your say-so."

Annabelle tottered around the potholes on Lolly Lane, doing a little dance as she first avoided one, then another. Despite the heavy rain of two nights ago, they still resembled moon craters rather than ponds, and they still presented a significant threat to her ankles. Annabelle had decided to make another pastoral visit to the brotherhood. She wanted to talk to Thomas about his mother and check on Sally. If she had time she'd speak to Scott about his argument with Theo. She couldn't help but feel that Ainslie and Lawrence were overlooking something important.

As she approached the gate at the end of the lane, the prospect of walking through the trees, past the site where she'd found Theo's body, began to trouble her. She started to mutter quietly to herself and jammed her hands into her cassock's pockets as she watched where she put her feet.

"Reverend!" Rebecca Hamilton was in her neat, orderly garden. She was hanging out washing. "I'm glad I caught you. Will you have a cup of tea?"

Rebecca was in her thirties. Her slim figure failed to fill

out the clothes that hung from her, wrinkled and shapeless, her auburn hair pulled up into a messy ponytail and secured with a scrunchy.

"Why not?" Annabelle replied, thirsty from her pothole dancing and keen to dispel her heavy feelings by spending some time with this busy, cheery woman.

They went into the Hamilton's messy and well-loved kitchen. Rebecca pulled out a chair for Annabelle only to find a pile of clean laundry on the seat.

"Oh!"

In one swift, seamless movement, Rebecca turned out a basket full of dirty laundry onto the kitchen floor and swept the clean clothes on the chair into now-empty laundry basket. She tossed it into the corner and triumphantly presented Annabelle with the empty seat.

"I'm guessing that's not the first time you've done that, eh Rebecca?"

"Story of my life," she said, laughing. Rebecca put the kettle on. "What is going on? The police have been coming and going for days. One said there had been a murder! Is it true?" Rebecca was a very competent mother of five. Nothing much fazed her. She seemed positively energised by this latest piece of news.

"Unfortunately, yes. Monday evening."

"Golly." Rebecca sat down and pulled the lid off a tin. "Chocolate finger?"

"Oh, no thanks, I'm trying to be good. But don't mind me." Rebecca didn't, and she grabbed a couple of custard creams before putting the lid back on and placing the tin on a top shelf away, presumably, from her three sons and two daughters.

"It wasn't anyone we know, was it?"

"Theo Westmoreland. Did you know him?"

"Theo. Was he the good-looking, charming one?"

"Yes."

"Oh dear, that is a shame."

"Did you know him well?"

"Oh no, but he seemed such a nice man. He had an easy smile. He always waved to the children when he went by. Such a difference from that other chap who lives there."

"Which other chap, Rebecca?"

"The dark, swarthy one, the one who works at the smithy down the lane and around the corner. He was having a right go at that Theo the other morning when I went past. Monday, I think it was. Pointing his finger, waving his arms. I couldn't hear what he was saying, mind, but they weren't having a friendly chat."

"Have you told the police this, Rebecca?"

Rebecca folded her arms. "Well, no. They haven't asked."

"Hmm, well, if they do come around, be sure to tell them, won't you?"

"Okay, Vicar, I will. I hope they get whoever did this and fast. I don't like to think of something like that happening so close. I'll have to keep the kids in after school. Don't want them roaming around with a killer on the loose."

Annabelle drained her cup. "Well, I must be getting on. Thank you for the tea. Much appreciated."

"Least I can do. You've got your hands full with that show you're putting on, but I will say the children are enjoying themselves. They're singing at the top of their lungs all the time. The only reason they're not here now is because they went to the Palmer's house to practice some more. Eleanor is singing in her sleep!"

"I'm glad they're enjoying it so much. I think it'll be quite a performance, one way or another."

"I bet it will be, Reverend. Well, I won't hold you responsible. I know what it's like." Rebecca burst out laughing and patted Annabelle on the back. She followed her to the door.

"Bye, Rebecca. Thanks again for the tea."

Annabelle hurried off, looking at her watch. Scott might still be at the forge. Perhaps she'd skip the big house and make her way to the smithy instead.

The gate at the end of the lane creaked ominously as Annabelle swung it open, and when it clanged shut, her brooding mood returned. As she got closer to the site where she had tripped over Theo's body, her heart beat faster. The summer late afternoon sun was low, but there were a few hours of daylight left. She could see clearly, but the shade of the trees and the swaying of the leaves brushed by the light breeze was unnerving. The memories of last Monday night plagued her, even as she tried to stamp them away with her feet. She rounded a tree.

"Hello again, Vicar!"

"Oh!"

CHAPTER TWENTY-TWO

THOMAS HELD HIS camera to his face. There was a whirring sound, and he lowered it. "S–sorry, did I surprise you?"

"Yes, you did, Thomas. Do you always go around taking pictures like that, jumping out and scaring people?" Annabelle steadied herself as she leant on a tree trunk to catch her breath.

"S–sorry," Thomas tried again. "Are you alright?"

"Yes, yes, thank you." Annabelle pushed herself off the tree and started walking again. Thomas fell in beside her. Up ahead on the path, she could see the white tent that had covered Theo's body two nights ago. Yellow police tape wrapped around trees marked the crime scene area.

"Are you going to have another l–look, Vicar?" Thomas nodded at the tent.

"What? Good grief, no. I'm walking to the forge," Annabelle said. "What have you been doing out here?"

"Just looking for a f–few good shots. B–birds, deer, voles, anything. It's a bit quiet though, today. Perhaps all the activity out here has made the animals go f–further afield."

"Hmm, well, I hope you don't jump out on them like you did me." Annabelle frowned.

"Sorry, Vicar. I can be a bit awkward –sometimes." Thomas sighed and pushed his glasses higher up his nose as he stared at the ground. "I know the others get a bit f–fed up with me. They think I have my head in the clouds, that I go out with my c–camera, and lose track of the time, forgetting to show up for m–meals and m–meetings. And that does happen sometimes, not as often as they think, but it makes me unreliable in their eyes." He sighed. Annabelle looked at him sympathetically. Loneliness was most stark when it occurred among a crowd.

"When did you start to get interested in photography, Thomas?"

"I picked it up when I was about f–fourteen. My nan gave me a camera for my b–birthday. I love being outside, just me and Doris—that's what I call my camera, after my nan."

Annabelle didn't blink. Fred Caravaggio at the coffee shop called his espresso machine, "Caesar," and no one seemed to pay him much mind.

" . . . I love the countryside and the animals, l–love being by myself. No one takes much notice of the p–person behind the lens, and that suits me just fine."

Thomas stopped and peered at Annabelle through his rimless glasses. After continuing for four more steps, Annabelle stopped too. She looked back at Thomas, who shied away from her gaze, and it occurred to her just how little Thomas wanted people to notice him.

"Is there something else, Thomas? Something you're not telling me?"

Thomas looked all around him. He fingered a leaf on the shrub next to him, avoiding Annabelle's eyes. She walked up to him and took his hand. He let the leaf drop and looked into Annabelle's open, earnest face.

"It's what Theo said the other night and what might still happen now he's g–gone." Thomas waited for Annabelle to respond. When she remained silent, he continued. "It's my mother, you see." He sighed and paused. He took a deep breath before continuing. "I told you that I used to live with her, that she got too f–frail for me to care for, that I put her in a home. I had to sell the house to pay for her c–care."

Thomas' voice cracked and he looked down at the ground. There were more deep breaths as he took his hand from Annabelle's and rubbed his palms on his thighs. Annabelle waited as he calmed himself.

"That's why I joined the b–brotherhood. It's virtually free to live here. I can do my photography and contribute to the group whilst being able to c–come and go as I please. I visit my mother at least three times a week. She's in Exeter. I c–catch the b–bus to visit her. The brotherhood used to live much further from here, and I didn't get to see her very often. It was like Christmas when we moved so close. I couldn't believe my l–luck. If we have to move away again, well, it would be very hard." Annabelle's eyes flickered.

"I don't talk to the others about Mum. I like to keep myself to myself. She's happy, and that m–makes me happy. As long as she remains so, and I can go visit her and do my photography, it'll work out."

"Why don't you tell the others your concerns? They might be able to help."

"I don't want them to make f–fun of me. They think I'm out shooting pictures when I go to see her. If they find out I've been lying to them, they m–might not like it."

"Why do you think that?"

"I don't know. I just do. The most important lesson I

learnt at school was that it's best to keep my own counsel. Safer that way."

Annabelle reached out and took his hand again. "Least said, soonest mended, eh?"

"Look, I've said too much. They're nice people here, good people. I'm the one that's a little . . . off. I know that. F–forget I said anything." Thomas withdrew his hand and clasped his camera. He played with the strap.

"Is there anything else, Thomas, that you want to tell me?"

Thomas looked down. He let out a big sigh. "I have a confession to make. I know you're not C–catholic, nor am I, but I think it would be for the best if I tell you what's on my m–mind.

"Okay," Annabelle said.

"After Theo died, I did something I shouldn't have. I–I went in his room. I–I got mad about what I saw in there, and I kicked a few things about." Beads of sweat formed on Thomas' brow. "I was so angry."

"What made you angry, Thomas?"

"Theo was always so m–mysterious. He had a tiny swastika t–tattoo on his hand, did you know that? He n–never let anyone in his room, and I was curious, so I slipped in Tuesday after the p–police had gone. He had all this Nazi stuff in there! My m–mother is a Holocaust survivor. The rest of her family died in the camps. The idea that Theo was a Nazi s–sympathiser infuriated me. My mother, my dear sweet mother, had been t–traumatised, nearly killed, and lost all her family because of people like him. I threw a f–few things around. I'm sorry, but I c–couldn't stop myself." He breathed heavily. "Look, I must go b–back. I'm hoping the police will let me out of here tomorrow. I normally see M—mum on a Th-Thursday. She'll be confused if I don't turn up." He made to move off.

"Goodbye, Thomas." He started to trudge towards the house. "I hope you get to see your mother again soon!" Annabelle called to him before the trees swallowed him up.

She watched him go, mulling over what he had just told her and its' relevance to Theo's murder. She turned to face the white tent once more and squared her shoulders. She would have to leave the path and cut through the trees to go around it. She gritted her teeth and, humming loudly to herself, continued to stomp her way into the brush and back onto the path beyond.

CHAPTER TWENTY-THREE

THE PONY COMING towards her was agitated. As Annabelle opened the metal gate into the cobblestone yard, the animal side-eyed her, and perhaps unnerved by her flowing, black cassock, the pony trotted nervously sideways, the whites of its eyes showing as it threw its head. The pony's owner held on firmly to the horse's bridle and to Annabelle's relief, brooked no nonsense. The baseball-capped woman clicked her tongue and urged the pony to "walk-on" as she heaved her body into its flanks for encouragement.

Annabelle flattened herself against the gate. It was at times like these that her city upbringing and lack of experience in country ways became obvious. Grateful that she had avoided a nasty bite or painful, trodden-on toes, Annabelle exhaled when the pony passed, only to be immediately flayed about the face by the swishing of a coarse, hairy tail.

"Oh, oh, dear me," she said, brushing her face and picking horsehair off her robes. Checking carefully to make sure there were no other large animals that might assail her, she walked up to the smithy's open door. The air temperature rose immediately. A red-hot coal fire roared in the furnace. Scott bent over it, his eyes covered with clear plastic goggles, his workman's shirt and jeans protected by a filthy, heavy apron. His hands were bare, and now Annabelle could clearly see why they were so red, scarred, and rough. He turned and cried in a deep, loud voice, "Out the way, Vicar."

Annabelle leapt back as he carried a glowing chunk of iron from the fire. He threw it on his anvil and started attacking the metal. Using the tongs, Scott quickly turned the burning lump over, hitting it repeatedly with the hammer, intent on working it into shape before it went cold and rigid. When the metal cooled, he briskly plunged it into the furnace to heat it up.

Annabelle flinched and blinked every time the hammer came down. Scott's muscular, hairy arms sent droplets of sweat into the air. He was concentrating hard, seeming to have forgotten Annabelle was there, and she heard a few choice words muttered as he shaped the glob on the end of his tongs to his liking.

Annabelle waited until he finished pounding the metal and had cast it aside to cool. He stood staring into the burning embers of his furnace, wiping his hands. She coughed. Scott ripped off his safety goggles and regarded her.

"Oh, hello, Vicar. I'd forgotten you were there. Um, sorry about my language."

Annabelle waved away his apology. "Mind if I have a look around? I've never been to a forge before." She smiled.

Scott swung his palms forwards. "No, go ahead. Take your time. Just be careful you don't trip. Smithies aren't the tidiest of places, and you could fall on something nasty." Scott wiped his hands on his apron and walked over to an outside tap. He washed his grimy hands in the cold stream that gushed from it, a juddering noise pulsating the pipework.

"Fancy a cup of tea, Vicar? I've sneaked in some cow's milk."

"That would be lovely, thank you."

Scott picked up a blackened kettle and shook it. Satisfied there was sufficient water in it, he put the kettle inside the forge on top of the glowing coals. He picked up a pair of bellows and puffed some air into the cinders, making them glow a deep red, giving them life.

Annabelle walked slowly around the room. It was dark, the only light coming from the fire in the furnace and the daylight that streamed in through the open door. The air was surprisingly smokeless, but it was dry and heavy. It made her eyes itch.

In addition to Scott's forge and anvil, there was an old, well-worn wooden workbench. Marks, cuts, and gouges peppered its surface. On the workbench was a huge vise, its handle laying in the two o'clock position. Strewn on the surface, around it, and on the wall were a myriad of tools, all made from cast iron and wood, some well seasoned. Annabelle couldn't see a modern, mass-manufactured tool among them.

"How did you come by all these old tools? I feel I've stepped back in time like I'm on one of those living history programs."

"Some I brought with me, but most were already here. It was like time had stood still when I arrived. I walked into a smithy fully equipped with tools that probably hadn't been used since the early 1900s. I couldn't believe it when I showed up. They might look old and worn, but you won't find anything near as good at any of those DIY shops in town. It's a privilege to work with tools made to this level of craftsmanship."

"What are you making now?"

"Ah, this? It's a fireside set. Shovel, poker, and tongs. They sell well around these parts."

"What else do you make?"

"I shoe horses, and the farmers often bring me their tools for mending. A lot of them have their favourites, often from way back. Even though they have all these new-fangled machines, they like their old faithfuls the best."

"What are these?" On a table in the corner, there was a basket of thin iron rods, each about four inches long.

"Oh, that's a custom order. For Brian Dawson."

"He makes doors doesn't he?"

"Yeah, he uses these in his hinges."

Annabelle continued to walk around the workshop, looking high and low at the workman's treasures that filled the room. There were shelves crammed with jam jars full of screws, screwdrivers, hammers, planes, saws, drills and their bits, files, borers, callipers, scrapers, wrenches, pliers, and punches. There must have been hundreds and hundreds of tools. Different lengths of wood were propped around the walls, cobwebs strung between them. Annabelle counted four ladders. Five chains of different weights hung from the ceiling, and various contraptions made from pipes and sheet metal bolted or welded together graced other parts of the floor.

"How long have you been doing this work, Scott?"

"All my life. My grandfather taught me. Being a smithy was his life's work, but my dad wanted no part of it. Pops was delighted I showed an interest. He taught me every-thing he knew. It's all I've ever done."

"Tell me again, how did you end up in the brotherhood?"

Scott took the kettle off the coals with a hooked metal stick and set it on the workbench. With his apron protecting his hands, he poured the water into two tin mugs, dropped in a couple of teabags, and stirred with a battered metal spoon.

"Sugar?"

"No, thank you."

Scott fetched some milk in a thermos. "Don't tell Julia," he said, his voice low, even though Julia was hardly likely to hear him.

After fishing the teabags out, he passed one of the mugs to Annabelle. He walked over to where blocks of tree trunk were piled ready for chopping into firewood. He pulled two out for them to sit on.

"Please, sit down, Vicar."

CHAPTER TWENTY-FOUR

ANNABELLE TOOK THE mug he offered her. Despite his best efforts, Scott managed to transfer his sooty fingerprints onto it. Annabelle blew across the steaming tea's surface before taking a sip.

"Theo recruited me."

Theo. Always Theo.

"I was living mostly off my farrier work, shoeing horses, but that's not really enough to live on, not even in Suffolk." Annabelle raised her eyebrows. "Newmarket, the race-horses, you know?" Annabelle nodded. She wasn't a fan, but she knew about Newmarket, the British epicentre of horse racing. She blew on her tea again. "Anyway, I'd make a few things and sell them at the local markets. That's where I met Theo. I wasn't interested at first, but he kept coming around and talking to me. Said I could do so much better if I lived with the brotherhood and that he could help me get more work, bigger projects like fencing and gates and railings for the big houses in these parts. It still wasn't what I wanted to do but, you know, needs must, and this seemed an opportunity to get out of a rut."

"What did you really want to do?"

"I'd like to work in films."

"Seriously?"

"Oh yeah, there's lots of money for metalworkers in the movies. Especially with all those historical and fantasy films, they put on now. They all need weapons and helmets, and armour. You can make a good living doing that if you know the right people."

"So why are you here in deepest Cornwall? We're almost off the end of the country. Surely the film industry is based in London?"

"Yeah, well, it were Sally who persuaded me. Theo gave up. At least he stopped coming round, and Sally started showing up at my stall instead." Scott's eyes softened. "She seemed so nice. I thought it couldn't hurt to join them, just for a bit. To see how they were. How they lived."

"And how long ago was that, Scott?" Annabelle looked down at the dregs of her tea. There were tiny black bits at the bottom, ash probably or perhaps tiny splinters of metal. Annabelle suppressed a shudder. "Roughage," her mum would have called it.

"Aw, see. Must be a year or so ago now."

"And you're still here."

"Yeah, still here, toddling along. Not going anywhere though, not really, am I?" Scott breathed in and let out a long exhale.

"That's a big sigh."

Scott looked at her. He was leaning with his elbows on his knees, his mug of tea between them. "Yeah, I suppose," he said. He swirled the tea in his mug, then took a swig.

"What will you do now?"

"Now?"

"Now that Theo is dead."

"I don't know, hadn't thought about it. Think I'm going to stop being a farrier, though. It's becoming too dangerous. I had a skittish pony in here yesterday. Wouldn't stand still for nothing. Kicked a bunch of times, right at my head. We had a hard time getting even two new shoes on. Had to abandon the job partway through. The owner took him away. Said she hadn't had him long. She'd bought the pony for her daughter, but the girl hadn't been able to handle him. She said if he didn't settle soon, they'd have to sell him on. She'll have trouble selling one like that, though."

"Hmm, that's unusual. People around here know their horses. They don't normally overreach. Do you know who the owner was?"

"No, but she did say she came over from Folly's Bottom. Brought him over in a trailer because he was too difficult to ride. I haven't had one that jumpy in a long time, and I've shod some of the most purebred horses on earth. The pony yesterday was just mean. The one I had in just before you came was no walk in the park, neither."

He gave his tea another swirl and threw the dregs onto the cobblestones outside. "Anyhow, Vicar, if you don't mind, I must get on."

Annabelle jumped up. "Yes, of course."

Scott put out his hand to take her mug. "Maybe now he's gone, it'll be better without him."

"How do you mean, Scott?" Annabelle looked at him, but he averted his eyes.

"Just that Theo could be a little . . . divisive. He liked to pit people against each other. Good people. Kind people. People who otherwise got along. He liked fooling them. It was like a game to him. He'd make them think he was all charm and good looks, then once they'd fallen for his game, he'd laugh at them behind their backs."

"You didn't like him much, then?"

"Hah! I didn't like him at all. Not that I'd kill him, mind," he added quickly. "He knew he couldn't pull the wool over my eyes. I could see him for who he really were. Mostly, he stayed away from me."

"Scott," Annabelle said, walking up closer to him, "I heard you argued with Theo a few days ago."

Scott stood and started cleaning. He began to rub down his anvil with a rag. "Did you?"

"I heard from two people that it was a furious row and that you grabbed him at one point."

Scott stopped his cleaning. He threw the dirty cloth onto the anvil and looked down at it with his hands on his hips.

"Well, maybe I did, Vicar. But so what?" He looked at her evenly. He shrugged. "My work brings in the most money, not that you'd know it. All the money we make goes into one pot. There's a budget for our food and stuff, and we share what's left equally. That's what we agree to when we join.

"Theo managed the money, but he didn't keep records, so we never really knew how much we made, or spent, or shared. And I think he used to take more for himself. Keep money back. I challenged him, and we got into a bit of a barney. He denied it all, of course, and the others think the sun shines out of his you-know-where, so they're blind to his game. He just used to slip and slide around, cheating us all, making us mad with one another. And he'd get away with it!" Scott's voice got thicker as he spoke. He splayed his hands. "Finally, it all got to me, and when he came here on Monday, I lost my temper. Yes, I got angry with him, and yes, I grabbed him. But nothing more!"

"So if you didn't like one another and you weren't doing the kind of work you wanted, why did you stay?"

"Because I'm a fool."

"You don't seem like much of a fool to me."

"Maybe not, but we can all be made fools of by other people, the right people. No one is immune." Scott stared into space before snapping back to the present, his attention caught by someone outside. Before she could turn to see who it was, Annabelle heard Sally's voice.

"Come to bring you some tea, Scott." Sally appeared in the doorway and smiled sadly. The gruff, grizzly man melted. His shoulders dropped, and he smiled shyly. His face was red from the heat, but Annabelle could have sworn he was blushing.

"Oh, thanks, Sally, love. That's too kind."

Annabelle took a moment to wonder why Sally would bring tea from the house when Scott had tea-making facilities at the forge. Sally's tea was bound to be stone cold.

"How are you feeling now, Sally? Do you feel better?"

"Oh, yes, Reverend. I'm much better, thank you. I needed some fresh air, so I thought I'd wander down to see Scott."

Scott ducked his head and brushed at his face. He turned his back on the two women and busied himself at his workbench. Sally walked up to him and put a hand on his shoulder, speaking quietly. He took the mug from her. Scott held it in two hands, and they chatted quietly. Sally laughed gently at something he said.

Annabelle couldn't hear what they were saying, but one thing was obvious. It hadn't been Theo who'd been making a fool of Scott. It was Sally.

CHAPTER TWENTY-FIVE

THOMAS DROPPED THE paper into the developing fluid. He watched it sink to the bottom of the tray, swimming from side to side like a stingray. He looked up at the pictures he'd taken. They were drying on lines that zig-zagged across the room. He peered closely at them.

Like many of the rooms in the big, old house, the window went from floor to ceiling, making it problematic as a darkroom. When he'd moved in, he'd taped layers of black paper to the cracking, peeling metal window frame, sealing the edges with extra tape to prevent chinks of light seeping in. He'd stacked a jumble of old clothes by the door, and every time he closeted himself inside the room, he stuffed the clothes into the gap between the bottom of the door and the floor. To complete the conversion, he'd tacked a rubber strip around the entire doorframe and rigged a developer's lamp to the existing light fitting. The lamp gave him a muted glow to work from, and he avoided switching on the regular light.

Thomas was never happier than when he was in his darkroom. He'd often wondered if he'd been a small, earth-living creature in a previous life, some sort of scurrying or burrowing animal. He loved being solitary, observing the daily interactions of everyday living. He enjoyed being unremarkable and going about his business undisturbed. It was what made Thomas a good photographer. He was unobtrusive and caught life on film in its most natural state.

Thomas was old-school. Not for him, the intangible indiscrimination of digital photography, the manic clicking that resulted when there was no downside to taking twenty shots where one would have sufficed. He composed his frames carefully, and every time he set his camera into motion, there was purpose and meaning behind his shot. Where other photographers clicked at anything, hoping for one decent shot, Thomas constantly searched for a composition that supplied enough substance to justify releasing his camera's shutter. He even enjoyed the cumbersome process of developing prints, the smell of the chemicals involved, and the way the photographic paper slowly gave up its secrets. The old photographic ways suited Thomas' personality: unhurried, restrained, methodical.

He looked across his lines of prints, examining each one in turn. One was of Sally hiding behind a tree. She leant against the trunk, her palms flat against it. Her eyes were closed behind her elaborately painted mask, her dramatic eyebrows testimony to her artistic ability and a steady hand.

There was a shot of Theo. He was running, his ugly mask incongruous against the rest of his clothing—jeans and shirt. Thomas had slowed his camera's shutter speed, there was motion blur. It trailed behind his subject giving him an eerie glow. It was almost certainly the last image of Theo alive.

Shots of Suki and Scott in mock combat were next. Scott's mood, indiscernible beneath his mask, seemed threatening. But Suki was laughing; she had no reason to fear him.

The final shots were of woodland nightlife. That Thomas had been able to shoot any at all was surprising considering the amount of shrieking and activity. It would have been understandable if the shy, quiet, nocturnal animals that lived underground, or in trees, or who clois-tered themselves away in the camouflage of the bush had stayed hidden until the drama was over. But Thomas' quick eye and low-key presence had rendered some nightlife nature portraits that were truly striking.

He'd caught a hedgehog, its spines various shades of brown and grey, strolling through the undergrowth, mostly hidden from view by a layer of last year's leaves. Its snout was lifted to the camera, its black eyes inquisitive and alert, Thomas had caught the perfect view of its dainty face peering out. In another image, a barn owl sat proud and serene on a branch, its white and gold colours blending into the surroundings, apparently impervious to the undignified revelries beneath him.

Thomas scanned the lines of drying images, silently selecting his keepers. He looked down at a print that he'd just submerged. The picture manifested before his eyes. He leant forwards, lifting his glasses to peer even closer, his face inches from the fluid's surface. Using a pair of tweezers, he moved the print to the nylon wire above and suspended it with a peg. He stared at the photograph again. Flicking back and forth between others on the line, Thomas' heartbeat quickened. He heard a noise and turned to the door, his eyes wide. A slick of sweat appeared on his brow.

The door opened slowly. Thomas didn't move even

though light streamed in from the hallway. A dark figure silhouetted against the light moved into the room and shut the door.

"You," Thomas heard himself say. "It was you."

CHAPTER TWENTY-SIX

ANNABELLE PUSHED OPEN the door to the Dog and Duck. Barbara was behind the bar. She tipped her head towards a solitary figure sitting by the unlit fireplace.

Richard Venables' slight, wiry body was wound taut. He leant on his elbow, staring into a pint, cupping his cheek in his hand. With the other, he methodically turned over a fifty pence piece on the wooden tabletop, heptagonal side by heptagonal side.

"Good evening, Richard. How are you doing?"

Venables looked up. "Who are you?"

"Annabelle Dixon, Reverend of St. Mary's." She stuck out her hand. "I was at dinner the other evening, just before Theo Westmoreland was killed."

Venables took her hand, but there was no enthusiasm in his shake. He returned to staring into his pint and turning the coin. "I don't remember, sorry."

Annabelle sat down. She could see Barbara in the background miming. She shook her head, no drink for her. She refocused her attention on Venables. "I've been talking to Sally."

Venables stopped his fidgeting and looked up. "How is she?"

"She's very upset. Her friend died, and her father was arrested for the murder."

Venables sighed and returned to fidgeting with the coin. "I didn't do it. They let me go." His voice was flat.

"You were involved in an argument with Theo. You threatened to kill him."

"Yeah, and? I didn't kill him," Venables repeated, looking up at Annabelle, his chin still supported on his hand. "I wouldn't! After they threw me out of the house that night, I just wandered around, furious. I thought I'd keep walking until I'd calmed down. After a bit, there was all this noise, people running around. I could see they were doing funny stuff in masks and such, so I walked away from it all. I didn't want them to see me and for there to be another scene."

"So what did you do between the time you left the house and when the police picked you up?"

"I just walked and walked. Those woods are big. I dossed in my car for the night, that's where the police found me. But I had nothing to do with killing that guy. Nothing at all!"

Venables pursed his lips as Annabelle looked at him steadily, her hands clasped in her lap.

"Do you know what a bolt gun is?"

"Uh, sure I do. I work in a slaughterhouse. We stun the cattle with them. I've used one for years. Look, I've been all through this with the coppers."

Venables sat up and tossed the coin onto the table. Annabelle gave a slight start. The man lowered his shoulders and pushed out his chin, before closing his eyes for a second. The life seemed to drain out of him.

"Look, I've got previous, from when I was young, alright? Since then, I've made it my business to get clean. Settled family life, steady job."

He leant forwards. Annabelle leant back, slightly alarmed. The way Venables thrust out his chin unnerved her.

"I wouldn't wreck everything I've worked for, not after twenty years, because of that twit."

He sat back and Annabelle relaxed. "But what about Sally?"

"Sally is my only child and that . . . that man stole her from me! Any father would do the same. That man turned her head and distanced her from her family. I was worried he'd take her money, but I was much more worried that he'd take her from us, that we'd never see her again. You hear such stories.

"She'd've come to her senses eventually. I just wanted it to happen sooner rather than later, and I didn't want her to be made a fool of. Her mam and me have given her everything. She's our precious doll, and it hurt her mam so much when she went off like that, without a word. Listen, I lost my rag, didn't I?" Venables clenched his fists. "But I didn't kill anyone."

Venables put both elbows on the table and hid his face in his hands, rubbing his eyes. A moment later, he sat back, blinking, his face red. He let out a sigh and regarded Annabelle with sorrowful eyes.

"Can you help me, Reverend? I've really messed things up, haven't I? I want to take Sally home with me, especially now, but I daren't show up at the house, and I'm not sure she'd speak to me if I did. What do you think I should do?"

"Perhaps you could give her some space, Richard. Allow her to come around in her own time. Let her know that home with you and your wife is a safe place for her. Encourage her with honey, not vinegar."

"Could you talk to her, Reverend? You seem to understand."

"I think she needs to hear directly from you, Richard. Quietly, no drama, no shouting."

Venables nodded. He looked down at his pint. "I could drink less, too."

Annabelle stood. "That would be a step in the right direction, yes. Good night, Richard."

"'Night, Vicar."

CHAPTER TWENTY-SEVEN

"THOMAS! THOMAS!" SALLY was walking around the house. The photographer hadn't shown up for breakfast. That wasn't so unusual, but when he didn't turn up for lunch either, Sally started to worry.

Everyone in the house was on edge. Now that Sally's father had been released, there was some relief for her. But the others weren't convinced of his innocence. And even if Venables wasn't the murderer, the spectre that someone else, someone still on the run, possibly one of their own, had killed Theo was creating suspicion. They were turning on one another.

The night before, Sally had intervened between Scott and Margaret in an argument over her smoking in the house. Scott said he inhaled enough smoke during the day, he didn't want to breathe it in at night as well. Margaret had insolently ignored his grumbling. Suki squabbled with everyone over anything and the tense atmosphere had caused Julia to take to her room with Barnaby.

Sally felt devastated not just by Theo's death, but also

by the unease in the house. The possibility that her father might be the killer made things worse. She found it hard to believe he was guilty, but things didn't look good for him. In the past couple of days, she'd confided in Thomas when she'd felt particularly troubled. Having gone for hours without seeing him, she missed Thomas' undemanding, comforting presence.

"He's probably in his darkroom," Suki had said to her, irritably. "Isn't that where he goes to be alone?"

"Yes, but he wouldn't have been in there for twenty-four hours straight, surely? He has to eat! Oh, I don't know. Perhaps I shouldn't bother him if he's in there. He doesn't like people disturbing him. The light ruins his photos."

"But still, if you're worried about him, you could just knock. If he replies, all's well."

"I don't know what you're so concerned about? Antisocial misfit," Margaret said nastily. "Maybe he was Theo's killer? Perhaps he's done a runner!"

"Don't be silly, Margaret. Thomas? No, never. He's much too sweet, much too docile," Sally said.

"Well, it had to be someone. Who do you think it was if it wasn't your father?"

"I don't know. I don't know! I can't imagine any of us here killing anyone, least of all Theo." Sally looked at the two women, anguish written across her face. They looked back at her, sceptically.

Outside the door to his darkroom, Sally pushed aside the curtain Thomas had rigged to keep his darkroom even darker. She knocked quietly on the door three times. Thomas was a quiet, observant man. It wasn't necessary to make a lot of noise to get his attention.

There was no response. Sally knocked again and called

Thomas' name softly. When no one came to the door, she turned the handle slowly.

"Thomas? Thomas? Are you in there?" Sally cracked open the door gingerly, unsure whether to go in. She put her eye to the crack. She couldn't see much, except . . . There! There was a puddle on the floor, the surface rippling every time a drop fell from the table above. Sally opened the door sharply and slipped in, shutting the door quickly. She turned to see what was causing the fluid to seep onto the floor.

Downstairs, Margaret stirred herself enough to help Suki with dinner. They heard a noise. Both paused their preparations.

"What was that?" Suki asked.

"I'm not sure," Margaret said uncertainly. They heard the noise again.

"Someone's screaming," Margaret said.

"It's Sally. Something's happened to Sally!" Suki replied.

Suki pushed away from the kitchen table and began to run. Margaret waited a moment. Then pulled off her apron and threw it on the table. She chased after her daughter as Sally's screams echoed down the hallway, getting louder with Margaret's every stride.

CHAPTER TWENTY-EIGHT

T HE EMERGENCY CALL came through to the Upton St. Mary police station just fifteen minutes before the end of Constable Raven's shift. Under normal circumstances, this would have caused a stream of uncharitable verbiage. Instead, Raven dialled Ainslie's number.

"Ah, Chief Inspector?"

"What is it, Raven? I'm just about to turn into my driveway."

"Um, sir, there's been another suspicious death. At the big house in Upton St. Mary."

Raven held the phone away from his ear when Ainslie realised he would need to turn around and get back to the village without so much as a cup of tea.

"Yes, sir, I'll get there right away. See you shortly."

Raven rammed on his cap and jogged to the police car. As he reversed out of the parking spot, he plugged another number into his phone and put it on speaker. Annabelle was pruning her roses when the call from Raven came through.

"Constable, what can I do you for?"

"Reverend, there's been another death at the big house."

Annabelle chopped the head off a beautiful red rose. She cringed. "Fiddlesticks!"

"I know, it's a terrible thing," Raven said. "Ainslie won't be there for another forty-five minutes. Shall I pick you up on the way?"

"Thank you, Jim, but it'll be quicker if I make my own way there. See you in a bit."

Annabelle pulled off her gardening gloves and ran inside. She poured some water into a glass and popped the cut rose into it. Staring at the bloom, she sighed before shaking herself. She trotted upstairs to change out of her gardening clothes but stopped halfway. She wanted to get to the house before Chief Inspector Ainslie. No doubt he would throw her out as soon as he saw her. Gardening clothes would have to do.

Annabelle's royal blue Mini Cooper sped along the road out of the village and along the lane to the big house. She spun the wheel to turn up the pitted gravel driveway, her back wheels slipping and kicking up dust in her haste. Righting the car, she kept her foot on the accelerator, bumping along the track and skidding to a halt outside the door. Her arrival coincided with that of Constable Raven, who had motored there at a more leisurely pace.

"What do you know, Constable?" she whispered as they walked in together. She was relieved to see no police officer on duty this time.

"Not much, the body's a male, that's about it. Woman was a bit, er, hysterical."

"Then it can be one of only two people."

"Oh?"

"There's only two men left here. Scott and Thomas."

Annabelle showed Constable Raven to the kitchen. They looked through the glass door to where the four women assembled. Sally was sitting at the table, a crumpled tissue once again at her mouth. Julia sat next to her, holding her hand. Suki patted Sally's shoulder whilst Margaret stood aloof from the crowd. She leant back against the sink, cradling a glass of clear liquid against her chest. She looked pale.

"Did you know they call themselves the 'Brotherhood of St. Petrie?'" Raven looked at the four women dubiously. "They don't look very brotherly to me," he whispered.

Annabelle shook her head, "It's just a name. It means they're a group, they're all in this together."

"They're in what together, Reverend?"

"You know, life."

Annabelle pushed open the door to the kitchen. "Hello Annabelle," Suki said. There was a tremor in her voice.

"I'm sorry—" Annabelle began. There were heavy footsteps outside and the kitchen door opened with a bang. Scott's large form entered the room, darkening it considerably.

"What's going on? There's a police car in the driveway and more in the distance. They're coming this way."

"It's Thomas," Margaret said. "He's dead."

Scott looked around the room at everyone. "What? How?"

"Sally found him."

"He was in his darkroom. Drowned," Julia said.

"No way." Scott stomped out of the kitchen and down the hallway to the flight of stairs that led to the upper rooms.

"Stop, sir," Raven called after him. "You can't go in there. I have to seal the crime scene." Raven chased after Scott, who was running now. Annabelle followed. Scott was fast, and Raven lumbered in his wake, but Annabelle had several inches on the constable and soon left him behind. Scott conveniently led them to Thomas' room, running down corridors, and skidding around corners. Just before he reached it, Annabelle caught up to him and put herself between the large man and the doorway, their faces inches apart.

"Best if you join the ladies in the kitchen, sir," Raven called out, panting from behind and leaning on a bannister rail. Scott glared at Annabelle mutinously. "It's for the best. There's nothing you can do for your friend," the policeman added.

"For Thomas," Annabelle said gently.

On hearing Thomas' name, Scott relaxed. He quietly acquiesced and moved away from Annabelle. He walked back the way he had come, flicking one last mulish look at Raven as he passed.

The constable walked up to Annabelle. "Quick, the others will be here soon. Don't touch anything and take as few steps as possible, okay?" Annabelle nodded. Her heart was beating hard in her chest. Her fingertips tingled.

"So it's Thomas?" Raven asked.

"Yes, it's Thomas. Thomas Reisman. He's been a member of the brotherhood for a couple of years."

Raven took a handkerchief and turned the doorknob carefully. Immediately, they smelt the metallic, acrid fumes of the darkroom chemicals. Raven reached for the light switch, but Annabelle held out her hand. She pointed to the safelight and the pictures hanging from pegs on the lines strung across the room. They peered through the gloom. A creak made Annabelle start, and she felt a cold sensation curl around her toes. She looked down. Fluid had seeped through the weakened seam of her old gardening shoes. Next to her foot was an upturned tray, photographs strewn on the floor. Lying face down was Thomas, his cheek lying on one of the prints. His glasses were on the floor next to him, smashed. His face was white, his lips blue.

Sighing, Annabelle crouched down, placing her hand on Thomas' shoulder. She closed her eyes and said a silent prayer. She looked at the prints on which Thomas lay.

The bonfire, sparks fizzing into the smoke, flames curling around wood featured in one. Another was of the stormy sky, two crows flying across it. But it was the print that lay under Thomas' shoulder that interested Annabelle the most. Thomas had taken a wide-angle photo of a barn owl in a tree next to a clearing, a fallen tree trunk to one side. The bird appeared to be looking at something but before she could take a closer look, a voice cut through the silence.

"What have we got, Raven?" Chief Inspector Brian Ainslie appeared in the doorway. He caught sight of Annabelle. "What are you doing here?" He glared at her.

"Man, about thirty, sir, Thomas Reisman. Been a member of the brotherhood for about two years. This was his darkroom. Looks like he drowned." Raven spoke in a rush.

Annabelle sidled past Ainslie and onto the landing. "Chief Inspector," she mumbled as she passed him. He paid her no attention, although she thought she heard a tutting sound. She hurried down the staircase and back to the kitchen where the four women and Scott still congregated. Annabelle sat down at the table, a little out of breath.

"What happened?" she asked them.

Sally stuttered in between tears. "I found him. He hadn't been seen all day so I went looking for him. Oh, Annabelle, it was awful. Poor Thomas, he didn't deserve that. He wouldn't hurt a fly."

"Do you think it was definitely murder?"

"How could it not be? You can't drown yourself in an inch of liquid, surely," Margaret said.

"Where were you these past twenty-four hours?"

"We were all here, except for Scott," Sally said.

"I was at the forge."

"You mean, do you mean, could it be . . ." Suki stammered, ". . . one of *us*?"

There was a bump and a shout from upstairs. They looked up at the ceiling. Margaret, who'd moved closer to the table, moved back to the sink again. Julia let go of Sally's hand and folded her arms. The atmosphere in the room got a little cooler.

"But surely not. It couldn't be any of us. I mean, why would we?" Suki said.

"Why would anyone? I mean, Thomas?" Sally replied.

"Wait a minute. Your father's out of police custody. It could have been him. He could have come back to finish the job he started," Margaret said. Julia nodded. Sally looked affronted, but she said nothing.

"Perhaps it's a random person from outside coming in," Suki offered. "It wouldn't be hard in this rambling old place. Especially at night."

"But why?" Julia said. "A serial killer picking off his victims at random? In Upton St. Mary? Really?"

Annabelle opened her mouth to speak but closed it again. The idea seemed utterly implausible, but after the strange goings-on she'd encountered since she'd lived in the village, nothing surprised her.

CHAPTER TWENTY-NINE

A NNABELLE BANGED THE garden gate shut and walked up the path as she shrugged off her jacket. "Philippa! Are you here?"

She sat on the back doorstep and leant over to unlace her gardening shoes. When she'd first moved to Upton St. Mary, she hadn't fussed too much about wearing footwear in the house but a few of Philippa's disapproving looks and barely disguised tutting had cured her of the habit. She tossed the shoes to the side where they would lie protected from the elements by the porch overhang until the next time she pottered in the garden.

"Philippa!" She opened the back door. "Oh!" Sitting at the kitchen table nursing a mug of tea was Mike.

"Hello, Annabelle," he smiled.

"Mike!" Annabelle beamed. "You're back! I wasn't expecting you until next weekend."

"I'm taking a break. Tomorrow's session is on 'Social Media and the Police: Tweeting Best Practices,' whatever that means. They're expecting me back in the evening. I thought I'd stop by and see the dogs. And you, of course."

Annabelle was still grinning. Mike was in his civvies, jeans, and a light jumper, his brown hair tousled in what Annabelle thought was a rather attractive manner. He scratched his light stubble. "I thought we could take the dogs for a walk."

"Yes! I think that's a splendid idea! I've got tons to tell you," Annabelle said. "Let me go and change."

"You're fine as you are."

"I'm in my gardening clothes." Annabelle looked down at herself. She was wearing a pair of old, muddy and ripped dungarees over a shapeless T-shirt that had once been emblazoned with "More Tea, Vicar?" but which was now so faded the words were barely noticeable. Her socks had a hole in them. Catching sight of herself in the mirror, she saw that her hair needed a good brush after a day of weeding and crime scene investigation.

"And you look fine in your gardening clothes. Come on, the dogs are bursting, and they don't care what you're wearing. Neither do I."

As soon as she had seen Annabelle, Molly had gone to the coat rack where the leads were kept. She was now patiently sitting by Mike's feet, the lead in her mouth, her brown eyes looking at him in appeal. Magic, like his mistress, wasn't quite so disciplined. He was running around the kitchen, his tail banging against the kitchen cupboards, giving the occasional bark and odd little jump.

"Oh, alright." Annabelle was secretly delighted to go as she was. She would have wasted ten precious minutes deciding what to wear. Dressing to suit the occasion was all so much *effort*. Magic followed her into the hallway, where she took his lead off the peg it was hanging on before tying herself into her hiking boots.

"Let's go to the moor," Mike said. "We haven't been

there for a long time. We can all have a good stretch. Lord knows I need it after being cooped up for days on end. It'll be light until nine. We could stop off and have a drink at the pub before going home."

"Sounds good to me," Annabelle agreed.

"I've got a map in the car."

"Oh, er, can't we use the GPS?"

"Nah, let's do it the old-fashioned way. There's nothing like using a proper Ordnance Survey map to navigate your way around a Cornish moor."

"Well, if you're sure . . ." Annabelle, for whom all the squiggles and symbols on a paper map guaranteed a lost couple of hours, surreptitiously checked the amount of battery on her phone. She slipped it into her back pocket. She hadn't forgotten the time she went on an orienteering field trip with her high school class. As the leader of her group, Annabelle had managed to get them lost on a cliff's edge. All six teens had to be rescued by the local air/sea rescue. She hadn't trusted maps since.

She got into the car, and off they set. They headed for the rugged expanse of granite and grass moorland that stretched for miles, famous for the wild ponies that grazed there and its collection of stone formations dating back to the Bronze Age. The dogs whined in the back, their tongues hanging. They were looking forward to a long workout.

"Shouldn't we follow the public footpath?" Annabelle said sometime later as she pointed to the green sign on their left.

"No, the map says it's this way. And the track, it goes this way too, look." Mike was holding out his map, peering at it and then at the landscape around him, squinting.

"Alright," Annabelle said. "If you're sure."

Mike wasn't sure, but he wasn't about to say so. They'd been walking for two hours, and the car was nowhere in sight. They walked on. The dogs were slower now. Having bounded and frolicked for a good while at first, they were tired but good-naturedly pressed on alongside their owners. All around them, the occasional bush, tree, and rocky outcrop punctuated the gently undulating moss and heather. Large granite stones, piled on top of one another in gravity-defying configurations, cast long shadows. They appeared ominous in the fading sunlight. Above, the sky was dark blue, the clouds long and wispy as though God himself had breathed them into being. For another hour, Annabelle and Mike and the dogs hiked, during which their stroll became a trudge, their conversation intermittent.

"Look, there's some trees over there. We parked by some trees." Mike was going by sight, his confidence in his map-reading skills undermined. They changed direction once more and headed for the trees, hoping that this time, they were *the* trees. They plunged into woodland, the treetops casting shadows on the ground, making it difficult for them to see. Annabelle looked up. The moon was full, the stars were out.

"Isn't this romantic?" she sighed.

"Romantic? We're lost in the middle of a bloody moor. At night. How can it possibly be romantic?" Mike shook out his map roughly. "Shine the light, would you? I'll try to get our bearings again." Annabelle sighed and stomped over to him through the rough, wild grasses. She shone her phone's light at the map, the beam bouncing off it so brightly that she had to squint.

"We wouldn't make very good spies, would we?"

Mike looked at her. "Spies?"

"Anyone looking for us would find us in no time with a light this bright."

"Well, let's hope they do because we are well and truly lost," Mike mumbled as he looked at the map. He lifted his head as he tried to fix on a landmark before peering down at the map again, seemingly none the wiser. "Anyway, we're not spies. Spies don't use maps. They have gadgets and tech, and oh, I get it, this is because I wouldn't bring the GPS, is it?"

"No, no." Annabelle pursed her lips and looked skywards.

"Well, you were right. About the GPS, I mean. I shouldn't have been so pig-headed."

"We'll get out of here, even if we have to walk all night. If the worst comes to worst, Philippa's sure to send out a search party in the morning. Say, I'm sure I've seen this tree before."

"We should be getting to a crossroads soo—Arrgh!!" Mike leapt into the air. There was a rustle in the trees next to them, followed by the sound of munching. Mike backed up, pushing Annabelle behind him until they reached a tree trunk some yards away. As they rounded it, Annabelle bumped into a soft, velvety, hairy snout. She gasped, startled.

A pair of big dark brown eyes, framed by long, black eyelashes, regarded Mike and Annabelle mournfully. The sound of chewing continued before the eyes closed and dipped to the ground. It was a chestnut brown moor pony, unconcerned by its company. The pony stood alone, but Annabelle noticed two more through the trees, one a piebald, the other a grey. They all had shaggy, long manes and rough coats.

"Wild ponies!" Annabelle whispered to Mike.

"Great, just what we need to add to our evening. Wild animals." Mike looked back at the pony warily. "Are they really wild? Like they could attack us?" The pony lowered its head to the floor to pull up more grass. It didn't look very wild.

"We'll be fine. Let's just not startle it."

Annabelle made to step out from behind the tree. "Stop!" Mike looked in the distance. Through the trees they could see two beams of light bobbing up and down. "Someone's coming!"

CHAPTER THIRTY

"**B**UT THAT'S GOOD, isn't it?" Annabelle said. "They can rescue us."

"No one coming out to these parts of the moor this late at night is up to any good, Annabelle. Trust me on that."

A car pulled up. The engine was turned off, but the headlights stayed on. A door opened, and another, smaller beam of light appeared. Annabelle and Mike heard swishing noises as someone moved through the bracken, the light swaying from side to side.

Mike, with Annabelle behind him, retreated as the light came close. The ponies were alert now. They lifted their heads, watching. A woman emerged into the clearing. The piebald pony shifted its weight, and the woman walked towards it, talking softly. She held one hand out, the other behind her back. The pony allowed her to get close, and she quickly slipped a halter over its neck, rubbing the pony between its ears. When she turned and walked away, a length of rope in her clenched fist, the pony obediently followed.

"But I thought they were wild!" Mike whispered to Annabelle. She shrugged.

"Let's follow them," she hissed.

They tracked the woman at a distance to a path that crisscrossed the moor. Parked next to a signpost was a battered Land Rover, a horse trailer coupled to it. The interior light came on to reveal another woman. Together, the pair coaxed the pony into the horse box, all the while talking in a foreign language, their voices low.

"They're stealing the pony!" Annabelle exclaimed, her whisper feverish. She got out her phone. "I'll write down the number plate."

"K-B-D-1-2-Y" Mike relayed. The two women clambered into the Land Rover's front seats, and the interior light flashed on again. The women were young, slim, and in their early twenties. They both had long hair, one blonde, the other brunette. They were focused and grim-faced as they sat looking out through the windscreen before the driver turned to look behind her. The car swayed as it reversed away down the bumpy track.

Mike and Annabelle moved out from behind the trees. "What do you think they are playing at?" Annabelle wondered.

"I don't know, but text me that number, and I'll forward it to the guys at the station."

"Let's get back to the car. It's over here," Annabelle said, looking at her phone.

Mike glanced at her, astonished. "The car's over there?" He narrowed his eyes.

"Modern technology isn't such a bad thing, you know."

"Well, why didn't you say something?"

"Because you were so determined to do it your way. And I was quite enjoying myself. Now it looks like we may be on the hunt for some pony rustlers, so it's all good. Come on. You promised me a drink. If we leave now, we'll get one in before closing time.

When they got to the Dog and Duck, a barman Annabelle hadn't seen before served them; a pint of real ale for Mike, an orange juice for Annabelle.

"Here you are, Vicar. I'm just leavin'," said Miles Chadwick. He was vacating the table by the fireplace. It was the one that Annabelle had sat at when she'd spoken to Richard Venables. Mike and Annabelle sat down, the dogs curling up under the table by their feet. They continued the conversation they'd had in the car on the way back from the moor. Annabelle had brought Mike up to speed on the two murders and the characters who lived in the big house. She'd told him about the angry confrontation between Theo and Venables and that Venables had been released from custody just before Thomas was killed.

"So, who has a motive?" Mike asked.

Annabelle threw up her hands and rolled her eyes. "They all do!" She leant over the table and spoke so quietly that Mike had to do the same. "Suki is in line to inherit her uncle's estate, Margaret was ashamed of her son." Mike raised his eyebrow sceptically. "He was a Nazi sympathiser and all-round bad egg. It's not out of the question she might have murdered him, if unlikely."

"Okay, who else is in the frame?"

"Thomas' mother was a Holocaust survivor. Thomas said he didn't find out about Theo's Nazi beliefs until after his death. But he knew about the swastika tattoo Theo had on his hand, so he could have been lying. Thomas might have murdered Theo in a rage or due to some misplaced sense of justice. He certainly admitted to roughing up Theo's room."

"But then this Thomas was murdered."

"Yes."

"Okay, who else?"

"There's Sally."

"She's the daughter of the guy that was arrested, is that right?"

"Yes, Sally was in love with Theo, but her feelings weren't requited." Mike pushed his glass around and smiled at Annabelle's use of the old-fashioned term. "It could have been a crime of passion, Mike!"

"Okay, okay." Mike put up his palms. "It's possible."

"Scott is in love with Sally, so Theo was his love rival. Perhaps he bumped Theo off to get him out of the way. They'd also had a falling out about money. Richard Venables, Sally's father, hated Theo for luring her to the brotherhood. Julia hated him because he turned down her idea of setting up an animal sanctuary. I bet even Barnaby the rabbit wasn't too keen on him. Perhaps Theo threw his carrot tops away or something."

"Alibis?"

"None of them have one. They were all either in costume, hiding from one another in the woods, or in Margaret's case, alone in the house."

"And what about the weapon?"

"So that's the other curious thing. Theo was killed with a bolt through the heart. They use bolt guns in slaughter-houses to stun the cattle. Venables admitted to me he had worked in one."

"Well, there you are then."

"But why would he admit it so freely?

"Annabelle, criminals aren't the sharpest knives in the drawer. You wouldn't believe what I've heard in an interview room. One told me he didn't have a mother once. He had 'M-U-M' tattooed across his knuckles!"

"But you see, Scott also makes bolts at his forge. They are on the table in the corner. Anyone could have taken one." Annabelle was still leaning forwards, pressing her forefinger repeatedly into the small oak table.

"And Thomas' death? What's your theory for that?"

Annabelle threw herself back in her chair. She raised her hands, her palms upwards. "He drowned in an inch of liquid, some kind of developing fluid."

"That would have taken a man, surely."

"Maybe, but with the element of surprise, I reckon a woman could have done it."

"Hmm. Well, I'd follow the money. Seems like Theo had a lot of enemies. Greed is nearly always behind a case like this. Jealousy and hate tend to be secondary motivators. Very possible, but not as likely. As for Thomas' death, perhaps Thomas killed Theo, and someone else killed Thomas for revenge?"

"I can't imagine Thomas killing anyone. He was a loving, sensitive soul. He loved nature, wildlife."

"Perhaps the same person killed them both."

"But why would anyone kill Thomas?"

"Perhaps Thomas knew something. Something we don't know about. Annabelle, look, I know you want to help, but you don't have to go around solving all the world's problems, you know. Ainslie's on it. It is his job."

"Do you know his sergeant?" Annabelle asked, pushing her brown hair behind her ear.

"Scarlett? Yeah, she's alright, good at her job." Annabelle held her breath. "A bit prickly, though. And she's always asking me for coffee. I have to keep turning her down, or I'd never get any work done."

"Really?" Annabelle lifted her glass of orange juice to hide the smirk that crept across her lips. They heard a shout for last orders.

"Would you like another drink?" Mike asked.

Annabelle hesitated. "No, thank you. Best be getting home. I've got a busy day tomorrow, and you've got to trek back to Truro yet."

Mike picked up their empty glasses and deposited them on the bar. "Thanks, Barbara," he said. Barbara was polishing glasses behind the counter.

"Oh, hello, Inspector, I didn't see you there." Barbara fluttered her false eyelashes in mock astonishment. She would have needed to be blind not to see the couple sitting at the fireplace.

"' Night, Barbara," Annabelle said.

"' Night, you two." Barbara winked at her. Annabelle pretended not to notice.

Five minutes later, they rolled up outside Annabelle's cottage. Mike kept the car engine running,

"By the way," he said gently. "I forgot to mention, I liked that picture of you in the mask."

"Oh!" Annabelle's eyes widened. "Oh!" She blushed, grateful for the low light.

"I thought you looked very mysterious and exotic. Rather beautiful, in fact."

"Did you?" Annabelle's blush was furious now. She'd wondered why she hadn't heard back from her brother. She looked out of the window and took a strand of hair, twirling it around her finger.

Mike draped an arm over his steering wheel and looked at her. The light from the street lamp highlighted his profile.

Silence filled the car like a heavy blanket, pinning them to their seats, freezing them in the moment. Neither of them moved nor spoke until Magic whined in the back.

"Well, I—I must be going," Annabelle said. Her hand darted around, looking for the door handle.

"Will I see you tomorrow? Before I go back to the conference?"

"Yes, no, maybe, I don't know." Annabelle was now in full panic mode. She yanked on the door handle. "Like I said, I have a busy day."

Seeing her struggle, Mike reached across her slowly and carefully pulled the lever. He pushed the door open for her. "I'll get the dogs," he said.

"No, it's alright, I can do it."

"Okay, goodnight then, Annabelle. Sorry about getting us lost," he said.

"Er, um, goodnight, Mike." Annabelle stumbled out of the car. As she straightened up, she paused. "Actually—"

"Yes?"

She turned around and leant over, looking at Mike across the passenger seat. "Tomorrow. Yes."

"Ten thirty? Coffee, perhaps?"

"Yes, um, see you then. Goodnight." Annabelle opened the back door of the car. The dogs jumped out. She hurried to her front door, knowing that Mike was watching her. He waited until she was safely in the cottage, and with a flick of his eyebrows, he drove off.

CHAPTER THIRTY-ONE

ANNABELLE OPENED HER eyes. She immediately remembered what today was. She clenched her fists and opened them again, shutting her eyes tight and holding her breath. She exhaled slowly. Today was the day, the day she dreaded all year. The one that when it was all over, she would treat herself to a long soak in the bath and a big piece of cake, maybe two. Except this year, she would skip the cake.

It was the day for Biscuit's annual check-up. And that meant wrangling her into her cat carrier. Annabelle knew it couldn't be fun being trapped in one of those baskets, but she had hoped that Biscuit would get used to it in time. But it would appear not. For in spite of many experiments, Annabelle had not found a set of conditions that placated her ginger tabby. Instead, the vicar had reconciled herself to the fact that it would be necessary to walk down Upton St. Mary high street at least once a year with a cat who was intent on the feline equivalent of screaming bloody murder.

Annabelle got up and went to her wardrobe. First, she donned a pair of heavy jeans and a t-shirt. Next, she put on a sweatshirt, thick gardening gloves, a pair of rubber boots, and finally, a mask that she'd borrowed from Andy Kedgewick. Andy was a champion scuba diver who spent most of his time in exotic parts of the world swimming with wildly colourful fish. Andy was a popular speaker at the Women's Institute. Annabelle wasn't sure if this was because the members enjoyed his slideshows of unusually-shaped coral reef or merely the sight of the good-looking, tanned, muscular diver delivering them.

There was nothing exotic about the task Annabelle had in mind, however. She knew from bitter experience that getting Biscuit to the veterinary clinic required meticulous planning and stealth worthy of a military operation. She said a little prayer.

Annabelle reached into the bottom of the wardrobe where she'd hidden the cat carrier the night before. Opening its door in readiness and hiding it behind her back, she crept out of her bedroom in search of her cat.

She found Biscuit sleeping by the radiator in the living room. Annabelle nonchalantly walked up to her, looking up at the ceiling, muttering to herself, as if Biscuit was the last thing on her mind. As she got close, Biscuit lifted her head sleepily and regarded Annabelle with disinterest. For once, Annabelle appreciated her indifference and walked past before circling back. Quick as a flash, Annabelle reached out with her gloved hand to grab Biscuit by the scruff of her neck, She whisked her into the carrier. By the time Biscuit realised what was happening, it was too late. Annabelle, in a well-executed move, dropped the lid down, fastening it securely before sitting on it to make absolutely sure Biscuit couldn't get out.

"Phew," Annabelle said, brushing her hair from her mask. A feeling of exhilaration hit her. She raised her arms in the air, her fists clenched. "I did it! And no war wounds. No scratches or bites!" Biscuit was mewling loudly. "Sorry Biscuit, it won't be for long. We've got to see Dr. Whitefield. For shots and things. You'll be fine. You'll see." Annabelle kneeled and poked her finger through the basket's wire before pulling it back quickly. She'd come this far without injury, best not spoil things now.

She heard the back door open and close. "Yoo-hoo, it's only me!" Philippa called out.

"I did it, Philippa! I did it!" Annabelle held up the cat carrier gleefully. She felt as proud as a toddler showing the postman her belly button. Biscuit was still howling inside.

"Well, that's a relief. Last time, I wasn't sure you'd get out of here alive," Phillipa said.

"Oh, my gosh, wasn't that terrible?" Annabelle replied. "I had scratches everywhere. And I had no idea how to get her down from that overhead beam. She stayed up there for two days, you know."

"I do know, Vicar. I was the one who got her down.

"Oh yes, that's right. You were very brave, Philippa."

"Hmm, I don't know about that, more like exasperated. The standoff couldn't continue. Anyway, that's all in the past now. Where were you last night? How's the investigation coming along?"

"I was stumbling around the moors with Mike. We got lost."

"I bet you did, Reverend." Phillipa turned away, a small smile playing on her lips.

"No, we did, Philippa. And we came across two women taking a wild pony. We think they were rustling. It was very strange."

"Hmm, that is odd. You're not going to investigate that too, are you?"

Annabelle pursed her lips, turning down the corners of her mouth and waggling her head from side to side. She raised her eyebrows and looked at the ceiling.

"Annabelle," Philippa chided. "You won't have time for your congregation at this rate!" Philippa pulled out the flour from the cupboard, followed by a bag of sugar. She opened the fridge and set some butter on the counter. She busied herself lining a cake pan until she could hold herself in no longer.

"And how is the Inspector?"

"What? Oh, he's alright." Annabelle flopped in a chair at the kitchen table, her diving mask pushed onto her forehead. She took a breather, basking in the euphoria of knowing her day's toughest task was behind her, and it wasn't even nine a.m. "He's going back to the conference tonight."

"Will you see him again? Before he goes back, I mean."

"I don't know, Philippa." Annabelle was a little tetchy. A vague sense of loss and sadness crept over her, like she had made a mistake or missed an opportunity, perhaps made a fool of herself the previous evening.

Philippa changed the subject. 'I'm glad they have that man in custody again. That girl's father. From the big house. The one Barbara was talking about."

"They have? No one said so in the pub last night." Annabelle thought back and realised that Mike and she hadn't exactly invited social chit-chat as they had hugged their table in front of the fireplace. An icy wave ran through her as she suppressed a shudder of embarrassment. Biscuit was letting out a constant stream of yowls, and now that the euphoria from her capture had waned, Annabelle felt the beginnings of a headache.

"They hauled him back in after the second murder

almost immediately. The chief inspector's convinced it's him, so they say. What do you think?"

"Oh, I don't know. Venables was very angry that evening, that's for sure, and he'd clearly been drinking. And he threatened Theo. But why would he kill Thomas? Thomas was a sweetheart who just wanted what was best for his mother. Why would *anyone* want to kill him?" Annabelle sighed. "Anyway, it's nearly time for Biscuit's appointment. I'd best get going." She quickly ran upstairs to change before returning to the kitchen wearing her cassock and clerical collar.

Annabelle stood in front of the cat carrier and gave a short, sharp exhale, her hands out in front of her as if she were preparing for a bout of karate. With a sudden thrust, she picked up the carrier, prompting Biscuit to let out a particularly aggrieved growl. "Come on Biscuit, it isn't that bad. Anyone would think I was torturing you."

CHAPTER THIRTY-TWO

ON THE WAY to the vets, Annabelle passed Penelope Paynter on her chestnut mare, Equinox. She gave them a wide berth, and Penelope raised her hand in thanks. Annabelle thought back to the pony rustling and the injured children at the rehearsal. She decided to make some phone calls.

"Pat? It's Annabelle. No, no, everything is fine. Tell me, I saw Tabitha was on crutches at rehearsal the other day." There was a pause as Annabelle listened to Tabitha's mother's reply. "Really? That's terrible." Another pause. "I know, but still. Give her our love, won't you? Tell her I hope she's can cast those crutches off very soon."

After the call ended, Annabelle phoned the Simmonds family, followed by the Crackers, the Rinkers, and the Trebuthwicks. Chloe had shown up to rehearsal with broken fingers, George with his arm in a sling, Nancy had injured both her feet, whilst Timmy was covered in nasty grazes. They all had a similar story. All had fallen from horses.

Annabelle nipped into a parking space a few doors

down from the veterinary surgery along the pretty high street that ran through the village. The cobbled street had low pavements that rose barely two inches on either side of the road. It was lined with stone mews cottages, some of them whitewashed, their square frontages unchanged in centuries thanks to their protected status. The restrictions on development that preserved the heritage of the village gave it a timelessness rare in a fast-paced modern world. Aside from the street lamps, cars, and fashions, one might think Upton St. Mary locals still lived in the 18th century.

Annabelle texted the information about the children's injuries to Mike, before hurrying to the passenger door. She reached in to grab the cat carrier. She wanted this visit to the vet to be over as soon as possible. Biscuit was still mewling bitterly. Annabelle swung the carrier around, and with her foot, she closed the car door, only to nearly overbalance onto the pavement.

"Careful, Vicar!"

Sally bobbed and stretched out her arm to steady Annabelle, who was taller than she by some inches. With Sally was Julia. Barnaby was with them, poking out of Julia's jacket pocket as usual, his ears askew, one down, one up, propped there by the fabric of Julia's jacket.

"Oof, thank you, I'm fine. Just taking Biscuit to the vet. She's not a fan."

"I can tell."

Julia bent down and made little clicking noises with her tongue. Biscuit immediately stopped her noise and leant forwards to investigate Julia's face. She sniffed the fingertip Julia laid on the carrier grille.

"What? How do you do that? She's been making a racket for the past thirty minutes!"

Julia smiled. "You have to have the knack, Reverend. Not everyone has it."

"Well, I wish you could teach me. How are things up at the house?"

"Oh, you know, a little sombre. We wanted to get out for some fresh air, so we thought we'd take a walk into town. They arrested my father again, did you know?" Sally said.

"Yes, I did hear something about that."

"I can't believe it. I know Dad can be a hothead, and I know he's got form, but that was decades ago. He would never kill anyone, let alone *two* people, and certainly not someone like Thomas." Sally wrung her hands and looked like she was about to cry again.

"At least we're getting on a little better. Now that Sally's father has been arrested again, we can stop suspecting one another," Julia said.

Sally glared at her. "How nice for you," she said sarcastically.

"How are the others doing?" Annabelle asked.

"Margaret stays in her room, mostly. I took her some supper last night. We hadn't seen her all day. She looked pale and tired, but she was alive," Julia said matter-of-factly. "Suki, is well, Suki. Dippy. The selfies continue unabated." Julia, sensing Biscuit was getting restless, leant down to click her tongue at her again.

"And what about Scott? He seemed very perturbed the other night."

"Scott's still very upset about Theo. Thomas' death has just made it all the harder. He feels so bad that some of his last words with Theo were spoken in anger," Sally said.

"Were they? I didn't know that." Julia was surprised.

"They were arguing about money, Julia," Annabelle explained.

"They also discussed your idea for a donkey sanctuary," Sally added. Her voice had a hard edge to it.

"What about it?" Julia was suddenly a lot more alert.

"Scott said we couldn't afford it. He told me yesterday when I went to see him at the forge. Theo and Scott did argue about money, but they agreed on the subject of your donkey sanctuary. Neither of them wanted it."

"Scott never told *me*."

"No, well, he, um . . ." Sally started to falter, ". . . also thought that you weren't, um, up for the responsibility. He said if you were so emotionally attached to animals that you needed to carry a rabbit around with you all the time, you wouldn't be able to manage, and the rest of us would have to help out. He didn't want to get lumbered with the work if you couldn't cope."

Julia took a long breath in through her nose and drew herself up to her full height. "Is that so? Well, it's nice to know who your friends are, isn't it?" Julia jammed her hands in her pockets, causing Barnaby to shift over. He seemed unperturbed. She stared at the ground, tapping her foot.

"I'm sorry, Julia. But perhaps he's right. You are a bit . . . well, fragile at times. I know you love your animals, but . . ." Sally trailed off as Julia looked up angrily.

"I shall have something to say to Scott when I get back." Julia strode off.

CHAPTER THIRTY-THREE

"OH DEAR, I'VE made things worse, Reverend." Sally looked imploringly at Annabelle. "Things aren't good at the house. We're all nervous, all on edge. Everyone wants the culprit to be my dad, and I feel stuck in the middle. I can't mention my doubts because if it wasn't him, it must have been one of us! I don't know what to think. It's an awful situation to be in."

Annabelle put Biscuit's carrier down on the ground and ignored the yowling that had started up again now that Julia had moved away. She took Sally in an embrace.

"I do hope things get cleared up for you soon. Perhaps you should go home, spend some time with your mother. I'm sure she needs you, what with your father in custody."

Sally pulled away from Annabelle and sniffed. "Yes, perhaps you're right. Perhaps I'll get away. I don't know how the brotherhood can possibly stay together after this." Sally pressed her lips together sadly, tears welling in the corners of her eyes. "I should catch up with Julia. I said too much. I'll talk to her some more. Calm her down. Goodbye, Vicar. I'll see you soon."

"Goodbye, Sally. Take care now." Annabelle watched as Sally walked quickly down the street, past the newsagents, the estate agents, and the new curry house. Finally, acceding to Biscuit's yowly demands, she bent down to pick up the carrier. She pushed open the white wooden door beneath a bright green awning that announced "Veterinary Surgery."

Inside, fluorescent lights lit up the reception area. The walls, like the outside, were painted brilliant white and were bare except for the noticeboard that announced the date of the next cat adoption fair, the details of several lost pets, and the availability of animal bereavement services. The tiled floor was white too, although due to the passage of pets, it wasn't quite as brilliant as the walls. More a shade of grey, really.

Annabelle didn't recognise the young woman behind the reception desk, her face so smooth it was shiny. But as so often happened, the receptionist recognised her.

"Good morning, Reverend. Who do you have with you today?"

"Biscuit Dixon, annual checkup." Annabelle lowered her voice. "Vaccinations," she whispered, pointing down at the carrier and shaking her head.

"Ah yes, here you are." The woman looked up from her computer. "Someone will be out to see you in a minute. Please take a seat."

Annabelle walked over to one of the chairs and sat down, placing the carrier on her lap. Biscuit looked around at her fellow patients and letting out another yowl, promptly backed up as far as her carrier would allow. Annabelle looked around too, assessing the terrain. Veterinary surgery waiting rooms were often fraught, unpredictable places, she found.

She caught the eye of Justin Case, an unfortunately named teenage boy who she knew had an equally unfortunate habit of occupying the only cell at the police station on a semi-regular basis. Justin was partial to petty pilfering, a tendency he appeared unable, or indeed, unwilling to curb. Faced with the recurring news that her son had stolen seemingly random items of zero value, items such as odd ends of rope, empty bottles, packaging peanuts, and the like, his exasperated mother would cry, "What for, Justin? What for?"

"Just in case," Justin would assure his mother when she bailed him out of a morning following the previous night's transgression. "It's my name, innit? Gotta live up to it." In this case, Justin held a cage containing a bearded dragon whose only moving body part appeared to be his eyelids.

Across from Justin sat Mr. Penrose, but today he didn't have his pitbull, Kylie, with him. Instead, a miniature English bulldog sat in his lap, its nose flattened like a boxer's, its pink tongue hanging out as it panted.

"New puppy, Mr. Penrose?"

"Yes, isn't she gorgeous? I'm thinking of calling her Clarissa."

Clarissa had a white snout, forehead, and neck, but the rest of her was brown. Her loose, wrinkled skin looked like an expensive camel-coloured overcoat, of a type generally worn by Premier League football managers on winter match days. However, in Clarissa's case, it was three sizes too big for her. Clarissa looked at Annabelle dolefully before her eyes dropped to Biscuit and indifferently roved away again.

"She's lovely," Annabelle said optimistically.

"Biscuit!" a voice called.

Annabelle stood up, pleased to be away from the staring reptile and the breathless Clarissa. "That's us!"

"Come with me." Biscuit started to yowl again. The veterinary assistant took the cat carrier from Annabelle. Silence immediately descended.

"How do you do that?"

"What?"

"Get her to cooperate. She fights with me constantly."

"Oh, you just have to have the knack. If you don't have it, you don't stick with this type of job for very long. Animals always know, you know." The veterinary assistant left the small consulting room leaving Annabelle wondering what exactly it was that animals knew, when they knew it, why she didn't know it, and what it all meant.

A few minutes later, the door swung open, and Dr. Whitefield, the vet, came in. Annabelle always thought Dr. Whitefield resembled a cow. He was huge, with floppy jowls and big, fat hands. All he had to do was take a black marker pen to his white coat, and the transformation would be complete.

"Good morning, Reverend. How are you?"

"Very well, Dr. Whitefield."

"Who have you brought in to see me today?"

Annabelle went through the same routine she had at the reception desk. The vet opened up the cat carrier and lifted Biscuit out. Annabelle stepped back in alarm, her arms in front of her face ready to defend herself, but Biscuit was as floppy and compliant as a sleeping baby.

"How do you *do* that?"

"You have to have—"

"I know, I know, the knack." They both finished together and laughed. The vet examined Biscuit, took her temperature, and gave her the necessary shots, all without drama or injury.

"I don't know how you animal people do it, I really don't. The fuss she makes on the way here is beyond comprehension," Annabelle said.

"How are things in God's world?"

"Oh, you know, heavenly as always," she replied.

"I hear you've been up at the big house, getting involved in that murder investigation."

"Just helping out where I can. Part of my chaplaincy, really."

"Isn't that where Julia Snow lives? Small lady, strong, loves her animals. She's part of that cult, isn't she?"

"It's not technically a cult, but yes, she lives there. Do you know her?"

"We vets all know one another in these parts."

"She's a vet?"

"Oh yes. It was a few years ago now. She had to stop practicing, she went off the rails, you know. It was a terrible shame."

"Oh?"

"There was this horrendous equine neglect case. Julia worked for an animal charity. She had to shoot over a dozen horses. Went off her rocker and had to retire. Disappeared completely until she resurfaced here. I was so surprised to see her in the market square the other d—" The door banged shut.

"Wait! Reverend!" The vet peered out into the hall. "But Reverend, what about your cat?" he cried.

"Philippa! Call Philippa! She'll know what to do!"

CHAPTER THIRTY-FOUR

"ANNABELLE! PHILIPPA TOLD me I'd find yo—. Hey, are you alright?"

Mike had been coming through the door of the veterinary surgery just as Annabelle was leaving it. She'd hit her nose on his chin. Deep, bone-crushing pain spread like treacle through her head. Her eyes closed, but she nodded as she covered her face with her hand. She lumbered over in the direction of her car.

"B—big house. N—now," she mumbled.

"But Annabelle, wait. Slow down," Mike said.

"N—no time." She reached her car and pulled open the driver's door.

"F—Follow m—me." Annabelle got in and, shaking her head very carefully to clear it, she started the engine.

"Oh, alright." Mike ran over to his car; it was parked a few spaces away. He set off a few yards behind her.

Recovering quickly, Annabelle raced around blind, hairpin bends, and shot straight across crossroads. Mike stayed close to Annabelle's bumper. He wondered where on earth they were going.

"Crazy woman," he muttered before pulling on his handbrake to effect the sharp right-hand turn Annabelle had made at the last moment.

They were on a gravel and sand path now. Annabelle's tires were raising dust as she bumped and banged her way along. The trees that formed the forest tunnel they were driving through opened up to reveal the frontage of a house that had once been magnificent, but which was now in a state of decrepitude.

Up ahead, Annabelle got out of the car. "Sally, Sally!" Annabelle banged on the door and tried the handle. When it didn't open, she ran around the side of the house and under an archway. Ahead of her, Sally came out of the kitchen.

"What is it, Annabelle?"

"Julia! Where's Julia?"

Mike ran up. "Annabelle, what's going on?"

Annabelle was panting, her head was hurting, and where her nose was, it felt as though there was a cold pancake on her face. "Julia. Julia's the murderer." She gasped and leant over. Mike took her hand and put an arm around her.

"But Annabelle, how do you know that?" He asked.

"No time to explain. We need to find her fast!"

"She's down at the smithy with Sc—" Sally stopped and put her hand to her mouth. She caught Annabelle's eye.

"Oh!" Annabelle turned to Mike. He looked frantically between the two women, desperately hoping one of them would explain what was going on.

"We must get to the forge and stop her, Mike!"

"Okay, which way?"

"This way." Annabelle made to retrace their steps back to the car when Sally stopped them.

"Scott has his smithy over near the old stables down by the main road," Sally explained to Mike. "But the quickest way to get there is that way." She pointed across the lawn. The gently sloping ground fell away. There was no way to see the smithy, only the general direction in which it lay.

Mike took off across the grass. "Are you coming?" he yelled, looking back at Annabelle. She wasn't following him. She had run out of the courtyard but gone in a different direction.

"This way, it's quicker!" she shouted.

Bemused, Mike skidded as he spun around on the grass to follow her. They were running away from the smithy. *How could it be quicker?*

Annabelle rounded a corner of the house and ran to another building set apart by a gravel driveway full of weeds. There, parked up against the brick wall of the garage, were two quad bikes. Theo had shown them to her the night he had given her a tour of the house and grounds.

"Surely not, Annabelle?" Mike said. Annabelle looked at him, her eyes ablaze now, all fogginess gone. "Silly question?"

"Yes, very," Annabelle replied.

"Do they work?"

Annabelle hoisted her cassock's skirts and climbed on. She turned the key in the ignition. The engine revved. A pleasant whiff of gasoline settled around her, not that she could smell it. "Yep!" She set her shoulders. "Let's go!"

Mike jumped on the second quad bike, and off they went, the big fat wheels flattening the grass as they bounced and bumped their way across the lawn.

"Stand up in your seat!" Mike cried out over the noise of the engines.

"What?"

"Stand up in your seat as you go over the bumps! Makes for an easier ride! Oh, and lean to the opposite side when making a turn!"

Annabelle was soon handling her bike like a pro, hanging off the side as she navigated corners and adjusting her speed to keep her wheels on the ground. But then Mike overtook her with a smart shortcut around a tree.

"Noooooooooo!" Annabelle shouted and increased her speed, regaining the lead as she jumped a bump. Gracefully she moved with the bike's momentum as it flew through the air and hit the ground.

Mike continued to snap at her wheels, but Annabelle held him off with some fancy feinting and devilish daring. She pulled off some moves that made him wonder whether there was something she wasn't telling him about her youth.

When they went over the summit of the gentle hill in front of the forge, the smithy came into view. As the bike's engines slowed to a puttering, the forge appeared deserted. They clambered off their bikes and ran inside. What greeted them pulled them up short.

Up against a wall was Scott, his eyes wide. In front of him, pressing a captive bolt gun to his chest was Julia. The room was cool, the coals in the furnace black and lifeless. A hunk of metal lay on the floor. Tongs had been discarded nearby.

Julia kept her eyes on Scott, her jaw clenched.

"Julia. Steady now—" Annabelle's voice was soothing.

"I knew you'd find me eventually."

"We can work this out."

"No, we can't, Reverend. What's done is done. And I don't regret it. Theo was an evil man. Evil! He refused to let me have the animals. He refused! After he'd promised!"

"Julia, please. It's okay. Put the gun down." Annabelle slowly walked up to her, stopping a few feet away.

"You don't understand! I love animals. I always have. When I was a child, I had more pets than friends. It didn't matter what they were—fish, rats, guinea pigs, birds, cats, dogs. I loved them all."

Annabelle nodded. "They are all God's creatures."

"All I ever wanted to do was work with them. I never considered anything else. And I did! For twenty years. Then . . . then . . ." Scott moved. Julia pressed the bolt gun into his chest harder. She growled.

"Okay, okay," Scott said, his voice trembling, his hands up by his ears. He stopped moving.

"Tell me, Julia," Annabelle said.

"There was an animal welfare call." Julia's shoulders slumped, but she held the gun firmly. "I was called out to a farm where a horse dealer had neglected his animals. It was horrendous. We were able to rehabilitate and rehome many of the horses, but fifteen of them were too far gone."

Julia's eyes were streaming with tears. She took one hand off the gun and roughly wiped at her face. "Barnaby is my therapy animal. I've had him since that day." She looked down at the lop-eared rabbit in her pocket, his droopy ears reflecting his owner's downcast mood.

"I had to shoot them all. It devastated me. I had a break-down and couldn't work anymore. That's how I came to join the brotherhood. I met Theo when I was hiking one day. We talked, he was a good listener, and I told him my troubles. He lured me into the brotherhood with promises that I could work with animals."

Scott moved again, and Julia pressed down harder with the gun, clenching her teeth as she spoke. "I grew vegetables and fruit and the like, but what I really wanted was to help the animals. I'm good at it, and *so* many need my help.

"So what happened?" Annabelle asked gently.

"Before I joined the brotherhood, Theo promised me that if I pulled my weight and showed my commitment, I could set up an animal sanctuary for injured, neglected, and old animals, ones that couldn't find a home. So at every place we stayed, I devoted myself to the group. I went out into the community, made friends with the locals, solicited donations, and sold our produce. I did everything he asked of me. We were very successful, but my dream was to start a donkey sanctuary. They often have nowhere to go when their working lives end and live in terrible conditions, sick, and neglected. But every time I talked to Theo about it, he kept making excuses that we hadn't enough room, or we hadn't enough money, or we were moving too often.

"When we moved here with all this space, I could see my dream turning into reality. I had more than contributed to the brotherhood, so I drew up a business plan. I envisaged the donkeys being shipped here from the continent, or Ireland, or other places around the country, and cared for until the end of their natural lives, safely and peacefully. We could offer open days, an adopt-a-donkey scheme, and school trips. I did so much work to prepare, to get him to agree, and he'd *promised* me!

"Finally, he said no. He wouldn't even consider it. He laughed. Every time he passed me, he would make *donkey sounds*. I just flipped. I had had it." She pushed the bolt gun harder into Scott's chest. "Theo was a nasty, mean cad who cared about no one but himself. The legend of St. Petrie and Lord Darthamort? Pah! He couldn't care less about being a good person. He was just out for himself."

"So you killed him?"

"It was easy. The hardest part of the plan was to make myself a Darthamort costume. It made me sick to do it, all that fur and teeth, but I did it for the donkeys. Once the fireside ceremony was over, I changed into it so I could move around without being noticed. With us all running everywhere, you couldn't tell there was an extra Darthamort dashing about. Besides, no one paid any attention to me. They were all running around like lunatics.

"Theo was too lazy to wear the full costume. He was easy to spot. I'd saved my bolt gun from my days as a vet. It was the one I used on the horses, but this time I used it on Theo. Seemed fitting, justice. Very Lord Darthamort-like, punishing evil."

"And Thomas? What about him? What had he done to hurt you?" asked Annabelle.

Julia closed her eyes as she rocked back on her heels. Her head dropped. Slowly, she released her pressure on Scott's chest. The hand holding the bolt gun fell to her side. She staggered over to a chair by the cold forge and sat down. Scott sank to the ground. They all watched as Julia dropped the gun to the floor and put her head in her hands.

Annabelle leant over and quietly picked up the weapon. Mike relaxed and stifled a yawn in the background. Annabelle had the situation in hand, he knew all he had to do was wait. He was only needed for the arrest.

"Thomas. Poor, stupid, silly Thomas. He got caught up in this by accident. I didn't want to kill him, but I had no choice. He caught me on film. I couldn't see well with my Darthamort head on, so I had to take it off. After I'd done the deed, I saw Thomas snapping away and suspected that he'd got a shot of me unmasked. He didn't realise it at first, but later when he was inspecting his photos, he saw he'd captured me in the background of one of them. I went to his darkroom, and he told me he knew what I had done. I destroyed the photo after Thomas was dead. He didn't even put up a fight.

"I thought that was it, but then I found out about this piece of—" Julia stomped furiously over to Scott, who put his hands over his head, cowering. "You betrayed me too!"

That was Mike's cue. He quickly slipped over and took Julia's wrists. "Julia Snow, I am arresting you for the murders of Theodore Westmoreland and Thomas Reisman. You do not have to say anything, but it may harm your defence if you do not mention it when questioned, something which you later rely on in court. Anything you do say may be given in evidence."

Julia nodded sadly, all her fight gone now. "Aren't you going to cuff me?"

"I don't think there's any need for that. I don't think you're going anywhere."

Julia looked up at Annabelle. "But how did you know it was me?"

"I learnt from Dr. Whitefield that you had been a vet and had had a breakdown, that you knew how to use a bolt gun. You had had a disagreement with Theo. I realised you must have disguised yourself in a Lord Darthamort costume to shoot him. But what really clued me in was a photo I saw in Thomas' darkroom. There was a picture of an owl stalking a rabbit. But it was no ordinary field rabbit. It was Barnaby. I could tell by his ears. You couldn't carry Barnaby whilst wearing the Darthmort costume, so I figured you must have left him on the ground whilst you killed Theo and gone back for him later."

Julia nodded. "Clever. I could tell you were smart. You even care about animals, in a way. What will happen to me now?"

"You'll be held until your trial and then jailed for the duration of your sentence. In time and with luck, you'll go to an open prison where you'll be able to work outside. You might even be able to work with animals. That's probably the best you can hope for," Mike said.

Fifteen minutes later, a police car arrived, and Julia was dispatched to the station in Truro. There was an argument when the accompanying police officer refused to take Barnaby into custody along with his owner. After a standoff, Scott offered to take care of him, and Julia acquiesced.

"Aren't you going too?" Annabelle asked Mike.

"In a bit. But first, we have something to do.

"What?"

"We have to return the quad bikes!"

"Oh yes!" Annabelle's eyes widened. She started to run. "A return match! Race you!"

Mike clambered onto his bike and roared off, closely followed by Annabelle. Scott came out of his smithy, cradling Barnaby. He watched the scene, the two of them on their bikes, retreating in the distance, their hands wide as they gripped the handlebars, their bodies hunched over. Annabelle's cassock flowed out behind her. She looked like a bat on a bike.

"How about that? A vicar on a quad bike. That's not a sight you see every day, now is it, Barnaby?"

EPILOGUE

"**A**NNABELLE!"

SHE WAS dashing down the corridor in the village hall. There was just half an hour to go to the performance. The children's excitement had been building all day. It was topped only by the near hysteria felt by Annabelle and the legion of parents who had volunteered to help.

In the toilets acting as the boys' and girls' dressing rooms for the night, girls were giggling and twirling in their costumes whilst boys were good-naturedly tolerating the ministrations of their mothers who were scrubbing stage makeup onto their faces. The makeup team was led by Barbara. The landlady had taken on the leadership role with relish and, to the surprise of no one, had needed absolutely no training in applying of thick, bright, overstated cosmetics.

In the kitchen, Joan Pettigrew the pianist was practicing her scales on the window ledge whilst the boys on electric guitar and drums, Nathan Mead and Sammy Burke, were warming up. The low sounds of a bass guitar and the occasional crash of cymbals rose above the cacophony that resulted from forty exuberant children about to deliver the results of two months hard work by singing at the top of their voices and from the bottom of their hearts.

Annabelle turned to see Mike coming towards her. He smiled.

"You're back! You're here!"

"Of course."

"You've come to see the performance?"

"Wouldn't miss it for the world. I know how hard you've worked on it. I'm sure it will be magnificent and heartwarming, and everyone in the audience will love it."

"I do hope so."

"I also wanted to tell you about the pony rustling, but perhaps now isn't a good time?"

"I'd love to hear it, but later. I can't think about anything but the show right now."

"I brought you these. A sort of good luck gift." Mike reached into his pocket and pulled out a small box.

Annabelle's eyes widened, and she took the box from him. Haltingly, she opened it. Inside was a tiny pair of rose gold crucifix earrings embellished with shimmering blue diamonds.

"Ohhhhh, you bought these for me? They're beautiful! Thank you." She kissed him on the cheek. He smelt of pine. "I shall put them on right away and wear them for the performance. My lucky charm," she beamed. They stood there staring at one another, their eyes shining.

"Well, good luck then." Mike swung his arms, not sure quite what to do with them. "Break a leg." He took a couple of steps backwards and gave her a small fist pump before turning and walking into the performance hall. Annabelle, clutching the small box, watched him walk away, an idea forming as she wondered whether she had the time, or the nerve, to pull it off.

The children filed into the room, their expressions shy. They twitched with nervous grins.

"Smile, sing your hearts out, and most of all, have fun," Annabelle had told them at the pre-performance pep talk.

Camera flashes popped, and Kevin Poulter, dad to Sharon and the videographer for the night, started filming. Parents, siblings, grandparents, uncles, and aunties had come from miles around to see the performance. The atmosphere in the room was hot with anticipation.

Spontaneous applause broke out at the sight of the children and continued as the musicians filed into the room. It was standing room only, and as the children took their places, they searched for their families in the crowd. Annabelle brought up the rear carrying her conductor's baton.

She acknowledged the audience, and walking up to the music stand, took her place in front of the children. The clapping died down and a murmur rippled through the room. The packed audience of proud parents, family members, other locals, and visiting clergy looked at one another in surprise. Annabelle was wearing a dress.

The lightweight shift in dusky pink skimmed her body. It reached just below her knees whilst tulip-shaped, three-quarter length sleeves ended at her elbows. A small band of white in the upstanding collar was just enough to mark her out as clergy. A pair of pointy, slingback shoes in a matching shade of pink finished off her outfit. The ensemble was modest, and pretty, and feminine. The solid shade accentuated her blue eyes perfectly.

The crowd was momentarily dumbstruck, but as Annabelle raised her arms to begin the first song, the clapping resumed and got louder and louder, punctuated by the odd cheer as the crowd communicated their approval of this new version of their beloved vicar.

Annabelle caught sight of Mike sitting in the front row. As the lights dimmed, she smiled at the children and waited for the applause to die down. She flicked back her hair and raised her baton, her new earrings glittering in the half-light.

They made it all the way through the list of colours! They'd been courageously carried by the fourteen-year-olds, Trevor and Abigail, but all the children were making noise on the long last note, most of them tuneful.

Annabelle had told the children to "la" or hum if they forgot the words, and bob their heads in time. Taking her words to heart, four-year-old Maisie bobbed her head like she was at a Led Zeppelin concert. She was in the front row wearing her sheep's costume made from many cotton wool balls glued to a vest.

Things had been chaos in Maisie's household earlier. Just before they left the house, she had become unhappy with her sheep costume. She'd wanted to be an angel instead, so her harried mother had compromised. Maisie had gone on stage as a sheep angel. She was now, in addition to her sheep costume, wearing a pair of wings and the biggest, longest, emerald green clip-on earrings in Barbara's jewellery collection.

After the concert was over, in appreciation for the child-free hours that rehearsals had provided and the amount of effort the concert had demanded of Annabelle, she was presented with an enormous bunch of flowers and two bottles of brandy. Grateful parents and enthusiastic locals crowded around Annabelle to personally offer their thanks and congratulations.

Sally walked up. She pushed an elderly woman in a wheelchair.

"Sally, how are you?" Annabelle held out her hands. Sally took them briefly.

"I'm well, thank you, Reverend."

"Where are you living now? I heard you all moved out and went your separate ways."

"Yes, that's right. Scott went up to London to search for streets paved with gold. Margaret and Suki found a cousin of her late husband to live with. We keep in touch, well, me and Scott do."

"And you? What are you doing?"

"I'm working at the care home in Mevagissey. I live-in. I'm really enjoying it. Elderly folks are so much fun. This is Eta Reisman, Thomas' mother." Sally indicated the woman in the wheelchair. The elderly woman looked up with rheumy eyes.

Annabelle bent down and placed a gentle hand on her knee. "So pleased to meet you."

"Eta can't hear you. She's deaf and nearly blind, but she has a lovely soul. Guess who lives at the care home with her?" Annabelle raised her eyebrows. "Alexander Drummond! They sit and have tea together most days. He's a bit too far gone to know what's happening, but Eta is as sharp as a tack and knows exactly what's what. She teaches me every day to be a better person."

"And how are things with your father?"

"Improving. I'll go home eventually but not just yet."

"I'm glad things are working out for you. I wish you well, Sally."

"You too, Reverend. Fabulous performance!"

When the crowd thinned, Mike came over. "Great job, Annabelle. I told you it would be fantastic."

"Your lucky charm earrings made all the difference."

"I'm sure that was it."

They hugged each other. Over Mike's shoulder, Annabelle's eyes widened as she saw Chief Inspector Ainslie coming towards them.

Ainslie was as big and burly as always, his trench coat flapping as he marched towards her, except this time he was wearing a huge grin. He was carrying Maisie, who had dispensed with her sheep costume and whose angel wings were now askew. In her hand was a bouquet of gladioli that she swished through the air like a light saber.

"Hello, Chief Inspector, I didn't realise you would be here tonight."

"Couldn't miss my granddaughter's star performance, now could I?"

Annabelle looked at Maisie, who was now bashing the chief inspector over the head with her flowers.

"Maisie's your granddaughter? I had no idea."

"Wasn't she fantastic? When she let out that "moo," I couldn't have been prouder."

As he spoke, Ainslie seemed oblivious to the fact that Maisie was attaching her earrings to his large earlobes and stroking his bald head. Mike, in particular, tried to focus on what the chief inspector was saying, but the sight of his boss wearing huge, dangling costume jewellery whilst his grand-daughter lovingly petted his head as if it were a small animal, made it difficult.

"Anyhow, Nicholls, well done on the cases. Both the cult thing and the pony thing. Glad to see you so committed. We weren't sure about you, but you put your back into those cases and got results."

"The murder case had nothing to do with me, sir. I was merely the arresting officer. It was all Reverend Dixon. She made the deductions, identified the killer, and got them to confess. She should be recommended for a community award."

"Yes, you're right, I suppose." Ainslie coughed. "Well, congratulations for apprehending the murderer with the help of your lady friend here." He nodded at Annabelle. "She might not be one of us, but I can see that the two of you are a team, so I'll see what I can do. I shall be recommending you for a promotion when I get back on Monday. See that you don't mess up, alright, or get distracted with, er, God and such."

Annabelle squeezed Mike's hand. He squeezed hers back. When everyone had left, Annabelle flopped down on a chair and fanned herself with a program. Mike sat down more carefully beside her.

"So what did happen about the 'pony thing?'"

"We tracked down the person helping the rustlers," he said.

"Who was it?"

"It was a vet in Liskeard who'd developed a taste for the good life. The women would steal the ponies from the moor, and in return for a cut of the profits, the vet would drug the ponies so they were docile. The women would clip their coats so they lost their rugged, wild look, then sell them off as children's pets. Of course after a time, the drugs wore off, and the ponies reverted to their natural wild selves. Nasty. Someone could have been killed. We've apprehended all three, and they'll face trial later in the year."

"How awful. What will happen to the ponies they stole?"

"Three of them are staying with their owners and will be subject to welfare checks for the next three years. The other two have gone to a horse and pony sanctuary near Tintagel. When they're ready, new homes will be found for them."

"Thank goodness. All's well that ends well. That's a big relief. And perhaps the number of walking wounded will go down."

"Look, why don't we go back to your place? Celebrate your success. I've got some champagne in the car."

"Do you ordinarily go around with bottles of champagne in your car?"

"No, of course not. I brought it specially." Mike looked at her oddly.

"Come on, then. Let's go." Annabelle linked her arm in Mike's, and off they set, Annabelle's heart full of triumph and anticipation.

At the cottage, Annabelle grabbed two glasses from the cupboard and joined Mike on the sofa in her cosy living room.

"I've got something else for you. I popped in to see my sister on my way home from the conference, and she gave me this," Mike said.

"You told your sister about me?"

"Of course! Your brother's *met* me." Mike placed a

white cardboard box on her lap. Around it was a pink ribbon with a large gold and pink bow on top.

"It isn't a cake, is it? I'm trying to be good."

"Good? You can't not be good. You're a vicar."

"No, I mean with my eating. I'm trying to eat fewer sweets. Slim down a bit."

"Well, that's a shame, because my sister's a master baker. She works for one of the top London restaurants as their patisserie chef. She'll have you knee-deep in cake before you know it."

Annabelle rolled her eyes. "Good Lord, I am done for."

Mike lifted the lid on the box. "I think it's time you were just a little bit bad, don't you?"

Annabelle leant over. What she saw nearly caused her to fall face-first into it.

The heart-shaped cake was covered in cream. Around the edges were piped red roses, whilst across the face of the cake were sprinkled tiny red hearts. A few more lay scattered on the cake tray. A chocolate arrow speared the cake, and the word "Love" was written in chocolate. The chocolate words were placed at an angle, supported by more roses on the surface. It was simple, tasteful, and elegant. And it shocked Annabelle to her core.

"It's made with buttercream. I know that's your favourite."

"Oh, Mike, you are full of surprises. Thank you."

"Shall I get a knife so you can have a slice?"

"You want me to eat it?" She looked at him in horror. "I'm not going to eat it. I'm going to frame it!" Mike raised his eyebrows.

"Oh, alright, but not just yet. I want to look at it some more. And when I do take a bite, just a little. Then you must take it away, or I'll scoff the lot."

"Okay, deal. I'll take it down the station. They'll inhale it."

"I'll save the decoration. You'll never hear the last of it otherwise."

They sat quietly for a while. "I wouldn't worry about being good if I were you," Mike said. "I think you're quite good enough as you are."

Annabelle turned to look at him. Mike leant towards her, and when their lips touched, she felt she was melting and on fire at the same time. Their kiss lasted ten seconds.

"What took you so long?" she murmured when they broke apart.

"You could have made the first move. Haven't you heard? Kissing is an equal opportunity sport."

Annabelle shuddered. "No, siree."

"No? Well, maybe not. But you know, you're quite intimidating."

"Me? Intimidating?"

"You're so *good*. And holy. And everyone loves you. And well, you're a vicar. I'm a divorced detective." Silence descended once more.

"You look lovely in your dress," Mike said eventually.

"Thank you. It's a bit more feminine than my cassock, isn't it?"

"Well, I don't mind what you wear, but I will say that cassock is a little off-putting."

"In what way?"

"Well, um, there's rather a lot of *cloth*," Mike said. Annabelle smiled. "Look, it's not every day one falls for a female vicar. I've certainly never fallen for one before. It's different, I wasn't quite sure of the rules."

"The villagers haven't helped. They've been placing bets, you know, and I think Philippa and Barbara have been trying to track you down. I overheard them discussing how to do it. They were googling you."

"I think they wanted to give me a talking-to. There's a pile of messages from them back at the station."

"And then there's your other female admirers."

"My what? Who?"

"You said yourself Sergeant Lawrence keeps inviting you for coffee."

"Yeah, but that's professional . . . Really? You think? No!"

It was Annabelle's turn to raise her eyebrows. "And, according to Jim Raven, there's Shenae in the canteen."

"The one with the piercings?" Mike dropped his head onto the back of the sofa. "Gosh." He started to laugh. Annabelle joined in, and soon they were laughing uproariously, Mike's arm around Annabelle as she giggled into his shoulder.

When they had calmed down, Annabelle propped herself up on one elbow and brushed the hair away from her face. She looked down at him. "Seriously though, I may be a vicar, I may have a flock and God at my side, but I also want a partner, a living, breathing person. At the end of the day, I'm just a girl who wants to be loved and cherished. I want someone supporting me, lifting me up, and helping me with the everyday stuff of life. And I will do the same in return."

"I'd like to be that person for you, Annabelle."

"I'd like to be that person for you, Mike."

They watched the last minutes of the sunset, the bright white light of the sun fading and turning the sky around it grey and pink before the glow disappeared completely. The dogs lay in front of the fireplace, the occasional sound of their tails making a dull thump against the fireside rug. Even Biscuit jumped on Mike's lap and settled down.

Annabelle reached to turn on a low light. Mike put his arm around her shoulder, and she kissed him gently before laying her head on his shoulder. She scratched Biscuit at the base of her ears. The cat purred. The dogs yawned and closed their eyes. All was still and dark and silent. Life didn't get any better than this, Annabelle was certain. Life, love, God, and dogs.

And cats. Don't forget the cats.

Thank you for reading *Killer at the Cult*! I hope you love Annabelle as much as I do. In the next book in this series, Annabelle goes on a trip! Literally.

A missing priest. Scandalous secrets. A reverend with a taste for justice . . .

When a French priest collapses at Easter Mass, the church suspects foul play. A missing junior priest quickly becomes the prime suspect, but not everyone agrees. Annabelle and Mike dash off to France to join the investigation where they find themselves trapped in a culture clash of hilarious proportions.

Annabelle may have a nose for crime, but she's got no serious suspects, and too few clues. And even the rich French food can't inspire her to crack the case. On top of all this, Mike has a puzzle of his own to solve.

Can he help Annabelle put this killer away before they strike again, and spoil his romantic plan for good . . . Get your copy of Fireworks in France from Amazon to find out! Fireworks in France is FREE in Kindle Unlimited.

To find out about new books, sign up for my newsletter: https://www.alisongolden.com

If you love the Reverend Annabelle series, you'll want to read the *USA Today* bestselling Inspector Graham series featuring a new and unusual detective with a phenomenal memory and a tragic past. The first in the series, *The Case of the Screaming Beauty* is available for purchase from Amazon and FREE in Kindle Unlimited..

And don't miss the Roxy Reinhardt mysteries. Will Roxy triumph after her life falls apart? She's sacked from her job, her boyfriend dumps her, she's out of money. So, on a whim, she goes on the trip of a lifetime to New Orleans, There, she gets mixed up in a Mardi Gras murder. *Things were going to be fine. They were, weren't they?* Get the first in the series, Mardi Gras Madness from Amazon. Also FREE in Kindle Unlimited!

If you're looking for something edgy and dangerous, root for Diana Hunter as she seeks justice after a devastating crime destroys her family. Start following her journey in this non-stop series of suspense and action. The first book in the series, Snatched is available to buy on Amazon and is FREE in Kindle Unlimited.

I hugely appreciate your help in spreading the word about *Killer at the Cult*, including telling a friend. Reviews help readers find books! Please leave a review on your favourite book site.

Turn the page for an excerpt from the next in the Reverend Annabelle series, *Fireworks in France* . . .

A Reverend
Annabelle Dixon
Mystery

fireworks
in
france

ALISON GOLDEN
JAMIE VOUGEOT

FIREWORKS IN FRANCE
CHAPTER ONE

AWAY FROM THE main routes that connected Paris, Reims, and Calais, nestled in a valley, and largely obscured by a cluster of oaks, it was mostly bad directions or lazy driving that caused visitors to discover the subtle charms of Ville d'Eauloise. Should a traveller ignore signs pointing to the glamour and bustle of far-off metro areas, and if they veered from the main road to take a narrow, rutted trail, they would find themselves descending a slope shrouded by trees, and on sunny days, dappled with light.

If they continued on, the travellers would, after a time, emerge from the forest to find a small village. From a distance, it appeared almost ramshackle. Up close, it was something quite different, however—romantic, mysterious, intriguing.

Monstrous, stone villas loomed tall. Separated by lanes and alleys, they cast shadows at all times of day. The buildings, some with turrets and crenellations, were dotted with windows, painted shutters, and flower-filled window boxes. But no detail nor decoration could hide their age.

The village was a study in history. The narrow, steeped

cobblestone roads provided shortcuts, hideaways, and surprise destinations. To a local, they were practical and of little note. But to a visitor, they were enticing and exciting.

On arrival, the visitor would be drawn to *l'Église de Saint-Mathieu*, the oversized church in the centre. It dwarfed the much smaller homes, and businesses around it. It acted as a focal point for gatherings. Every small alleyway and lane led to the plaza that lay in front of the church. Local cafés, a restaurant, and stores ringed it on all sides. It was as if the village lived in supplication to God, his holiness, his spirit, his love.

But travellers rarely ignored the draw of the cities and only occasionally made the rickety journey off the main highway. For the most part, life in the village followed patterns and rhythms set in place long ago and performed with the consistency of a grandfather clock.

Inside the sombre, cavernous interior of *l'Église de Saint-Mathieu*, the stained glass windows amplified light streaming through them. The bright, mid-morning sun disseminated the jewel-toned rays on to pews, chipped stone walls, and shiny memorial plaques commemorating local lives lost in gold leaf.

Today, the medieval church was decorated further. Broad white ribbons wrapped around four pillars brightened the space. Delicate arrangements of white flowers softened the grey stone. Down the aisle, a thick, crimson carpet cloaked flagstones as jagged and irregular as the day they were laid.

The smell of melted wax filled the atmosphere. Even the crisp, spring morning air felt warm and dense inside the cool walls. An elaborately carved altar table draped in white linen stood beneath stained glass featuring pilgrims on horseback.

An infinite number of lighted candles emitted smoke upwards and provided an aura of calm. Absent the odd flicker from a candle's flame, there was silence and stillness. Everything was set. It was time.

To get your copy of *Fireworks in France* visit the link below:
https://www.alisongolden.com/fireworks-in-france

REVERENTIAL RECIPES

Continue on to check
out the recipes for
goodies featured in
this book...

LOVELY LEMON TART

For the base
6 oz (170g) digestive biscuits or graham crackers, crushed
3 oz (85g) butter, melted
1 oz (30g) brown sugar

For the filling
3 tbsp corn flour/starch
⅓ pint (150ml) water
Finely grated rind of 2 lemons
¼ pint (120ml) lemon juice
3 oz (85g) sugar
2 egg yolks

Pre-heat the oven to 140°C/275°F/Gas mark 1.

Place the biscuit/graham cracker crumbs in a bowl and work in the melted butter and brown sugar.

Use this mixture to line the base of an 20cm/8-inch flan ring. Place in the fridge to set firm while making the filling.

To prepare the filling, mix the cornflour and water together in a saucepan. Add the lemon rind and juice and bring slowly to the boil, stirring constantly with a wooden spoon. Simmer gently until the mixture thickens, then remove from the heat and stir in the sugar.

Leave to cool slightly, then beat in the egg yolks. Pour this mixture into the chilled biscuit base.

Bake in a very cool oven for 30 minutes.

PIOUS PLUM & ALMOND CRUMBLE

2 oz (55g) butter
4 oz (115g) soft white breadcrumbs
2 oz (55g) soft brown sugar
2 oz (55g) flaked almonds
½ tsp ground cinnamon
1 lb (450g) plums, stoned and lightly poached
Heavy whipping or double cream,
whipped to serve

Preheat the oven to 180°C/350 °F/Gas mark 4.

Melt the butter in a pan. Stir in the breadcrumbs, sugar, almonds and cinnamon.

Put the plums in a pie dish, then sprinkle the breadcrumb mixture over the top.

Bake in a preheated oven for 30-35 minutes.

Serve cold with the cream.

Serves 4.

Note

This is a very versatile recipe with many variations. The

plums can be substituted with lightly poached apples or rhubarb and instead of flaked almonds, try using chipped walnuts or Brazil nuts.

REFORMED RHUBARB FLAN

6 oz (170g) general purpose/plain flour, sifted
3 oz (85g) white cooking fat or lard
2-3 tbsp water
1 lb (450g) rhubarb, cut into 1-inch lengths
1 egg
6 oz (170g) sugar
1 oz (30g) corn flour/starch
1 oz (30g) butter
Grated rind of 1 lemon
Juice of 1 lemon made up to ¼ pint (120ml) with water

Preheat the oven to 180°C/350°F/Gas mark 4.

Put the flour into a bowl and rub in the fat until the mixture resembles breadcrumbs. Add the water and mix to a soft dough. Chill for 30 minutes.

Roll out the pastry and line a 25cm/10-inch flan tin. Arrange the rhubarb in circles in the flan tin.

Put the egg, sugar, corn flour/starch, butter, lemon rind, lemon juice, and water in a pan. Bring to the boil slowly, stirring all the time.

Spread the lemon mixture over the rhubarb. Place in the preheated oven for 30 minutes, then increase the heat to 200°C/400°F/Gas mark 5 for a further 15 minutes. Serve warm.

Variation

This flan can be made with orange instead of lemon. Follow the recipe but reduce the amount of sugar to 4 oz (115g) and add ½ teaspoon ground ginger, if preferred.

SOULFUL SCONES

For the scones
6 oz (170g) general purpose/plain flour
½ tsp salt
4 tsp baking powder
2 tsp ground almonds
2 oz (60g) butter, cut into chunks
2 oz (60g) golden raisins/sultanas
¼ pint (120ml) milk
A few drops of almond extract/essence
Milk, to glaze

Additions to make a 'cream tea'
Clotted cream (usually from Devon or Cornwall)
or whipped double cream
Strawberry jam

These scones are delicious to eat just simply
buttered, or you can make a real Cornish cream
tea out of them by spreading with butter, then

strawberry jam, and topping with clotted or lightly whipped double cream.

Preheat the oven to 200°C/400°F/Gas Mark 6. Sift flour, salt and baking powder together in a bowl, then stir in the ground almonds.

Add the butter, and rub it in until the mixture resembles fine breadcrumbs then add the golden raisins/sultanas.

Make a well in the centre of the mixture, and pour in the milk and almond extract/essence. Mix lightly with a wooden spoon or fork until a soft dough is formed.

Turn the dough on to a floured board and knead gently until smooth. Roll out the dough to 1.2cm/½-inch thick and cut into rounds with a 6cm/2 ½-inch cutter.

Place the scones on a lightly greased baking sheet, and brush the tops gently with milk.

Bake in the oven for 7-10 minutes, or until the scones are well risen and golden brown. Remove from the oven and cool on a wire tray.

All ingredients are available from your local store or online retailer.

You can find printable versions of these recipes at
www.alisongolden.com/kcrecipes

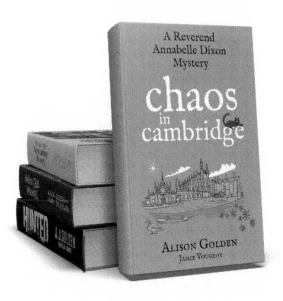

"Your emails seem to come on days when I need to read them because they are so upbeat."
- Linda W -

For a limited time, you can get the first books in each of my series - *Chaos in Cambridge, Hunted* (exclusively for subscribers - not available anywhere else), *The Case of the Screaming Beauty, and Mardi Gras Madness* - plus updates about new releases, promotions, and other Insider exclusives, by signing up for my mailing list at:

https://www.alisongolden.com/annabelle

TAKE MY QUIZ

What kind of mystery reader are you? Take my thirty second quiz to find out!

https://www.alisongolden.com/quiz

BOOKS IN THE REVEREND ANNABELLE DIXON SERIES

Fireworks in France

ALSO BY ALISON GOLDEN

FEATURING INSPECTOR DAVID GRAHAM

The Case of the Screaming Beauty

The Case of the Hidden Flame

The Case of the Fallen Hero

The Case of the Broken Doll

The Case of the Missing Letter

The Case of the Pretty Lady

The Case of the Forsaken Child

The Case of Sampson's Leap

The Case of the Uncommon Witness

FEATURING ROXY REINHARDT

Mardi Gras Madness

New Orleans Nightmare

Louisiana Lies

Cajun Catastrophe

As A. J. Golden

FEATURING DIANA HUNTER

Hunted (Prequel)

Snatched

Stolen

Chopped

Exposed

ABOUT THE AUTHOR

Alison Golden is the *USA Today* bestselling author of the Inspector David Graham mysteries, a traditional British detective series, and two cozy mystery series featuring main characters Reverend Annabelle Dixon and Roxy Reinhardt. As A. J. Golden, she writes the Diana Hunter thriller series.

Alison was raised in Bedfordshire, England. Her aim is to write stories that are designed to entertain, amuse, and calm. Her approach is to combine creative ideas with excellent writing and edit, edit, edit. Alison's mission is simple: To write excellent books that have readers clamouring for more.

Alison is based in the San Francisco Bay Area with her husband and twin sons. She splits her time between London and San Francisco.

For up-to-date promotions and release dates of upcoming books, sign up for the latest news here: https://alisongolden.com/annabelle.

For more information:
www.alisongolden.com
alison@alisongolden.com

facebook.com/alisongolden.books

twitter.com/alisonjgolden

instagram.com/alisonjgolden

THANK YOU

Thank you for taking the time to read *Killer at the Cult*. If you enjoyed it, please consider telling your friends or posting a short review. Word of mouth is an author's best friend and very much appreciated.

Thank you,

Made in United States
Orlando, FL
24 March 2024

45114450R00169